Naguib Mahfouz

Naguib Mahfouz

His Life and Times

Rasheed El-Enany

THE AMERICAN UNIVERSITY IN CAIRO PRESS

Published in Egypt in 2007 by
The American University in Cairo Press
113 Sharia Kasr el Aini, Cairo, Egypt
www.aucpress.com

This edition published by arrangement with Haus Publishing Limited

Dar el Kutub No. 10186/07
ISBN 978 977 416 128 5

Dar el Kutub Cataloging-in-Publication Data

El-Enany, Rasheed
    Naguib Mahfouz: His Life and Times / Rasheed El-Enany.—Cairo: The
American University in Cairo Press, 2007
    p.   cm.
    ISBN 977 416 128 9
    1. Mahfouz, Naguib, 1911–2006 2. Authors, Arab—Egypt
    I. Title
    928.162

1 2 3 4 5 6 7 8 9 10   12 11 10 09 08 07

Printed in Egypt

Contents

Preface and Acknowledgements

When my comprehensive study, *Naguib Mahfouz: the Pursuit of Meaning*, was published by Routledge in 1993, Mahfouz was already 82 and frail, had won the Nobel Prize for Literature and already written what turned out to have been his last novel, *Qushtumur Café*, in 1988, and I thought my book would more or less remain comprehensive and up to date. I was wrong. Mahfouz still had 13 years to live, and the flame of creative genius was to continue to burn bright until his very last days, taking his work in ever new directions in form, technique and style. His writing in the 1990s and until his death in 2006 was characterised by a lyrical pithiness that defied classification under known prose genres and styles; a mystical profundity able to distil life's wisdom in a few words, an image, a metaphorical situation, or a very short parabolic narrative. Old Mahfouz was vintage Mahfouz *par excellence*.

Naturally for Mahfouz's work up to the end of the 1980s, I have relied in no small measure on my earlier extensive study of the author mentioned above. And it is to that work that I would refer readers interested in a more detailed examination of the work of Mahfouz pre-1990. I have followed here a structure which sticks largely to the chronology of Mahfouz's *oeuvre*, while not refraining from disrupting that chronology on occasion for the higher purpose of maintaining thematic cohesion of the treatment, or to highlight continuity in the novelist's preoccupations and techniques across stages of his career. The occasional imbalance in the space given to the discussion of individual works is intentional. It is reflective of the status of such works in Mahfouz's *oeuvre*, e.g. the many pages devoted to *The Cairo Trilogy* and *The Harafish* against some novels being wrapped up in a few lines. For simplification for the general reader who now has as much, if not more, claim to Mahfouz as the specialist in Arabic literature, I have chosen not to use transliteration diacritics for Arabic names, words and book titles. I am confident however that Arabists and specialist readers will be able to work those out for themselves.

I am grateful to the Georg-Eckert-Institut für internationale Schulbuchforschung in Braunschweig in Germany for providing me with space, facilities and a warm collegial environment as Visiting Professor in the summer of 2007, which allowed me to focus uninterrupted on the production of this text. I am equally grateful to my colleague, Professor Rob Gleave, at the Institute of Arab and Islamic Studies at the University of Exeter, who graciously agreed to take on the burden of directorship of the Institute during my absence. Without his generosity it would not have been possible to complete the book in the time I have. For their enthusiasm and promptness, much appreciation goes to colleagues at the American University in Cairo Press, especially Neil Hewison, who would rush me by special courier at the drop of an email request the latest of their Mahfouz publications. Much gratitude is also owed to relatives and friends, Magdi Hamamsi, Tag al-Din al-Sahli, Evalyn Shalash and Shahira Samy, for constantly supplying me with valuable relevant books. Finally, to Wafa, and to our children Sonia, Nadine and Sami, for their love and support, I owe as always more than I can say in words.

Rasheed El-Enany
Braunschweig, September 2007

The Writer, the Time and the Place

Childhood and first love

On 11 December 1911, in the Jamaliyya quarter in the heart of the old city of Cairo, Naguib Mahfouz was born. Though he only lived there up to the age of 12 (in 1924 his family moved to the then new Cairo suburb of Abbasiyya), Jamaliyya continued to be a haunt for his creative imagination until the end of his life. Most of the novels of his early realistic period are set in Jamaliyya, notably *Midaq Alley* and *The Cairo Trilogy*, while in later works such as *Children of the Alley, Fountain and Tomb, The Harafish* and many others, though not mentioned by name and not recreated with the same meticulous detail as before, Jamaliyya continues to infuse his work in various guises and lends to it many of its typical characters and physical assets. The *hara* (plebeian street/quarter) with its warring *futuwwas* (thugs) and their gangs, its mystery-enveloped *takiyya* (dervish-house), its *qabw* (dark vault or arch which once housed a city gate), its ancient *sabil* (drinking-fountain), its shops, its café and the adjacent *qarafa* (cemetery) – all these components which make up the distinctive features of much of Mahfouz's work in the last 30-odd years of his life originate in the old quarter of Jamaliyya whose images were indelibly impressed on his consciousness during his childhood years. Mahfouz himself stresses the importance of Jamaliyya, or 'the world of *hara*' as he refers to it sometimes, as a source of inspiration for his work throughout his creative life: *It seems to me that* [a man of letters] *must have a tie with a certain place or a certain object to form a point of departure for his emotions.*[1] Mahfouz's dependence on the *hara* world as a background for his fiction and a medium for rendering his vision of man and society increased noticeably in his old age, particularly from the mid-1970s onwards. He explains this aptly: *With the advancement of age one realises that his origin is his true refuge … In the tumult of this strange world, one takes refuge in his childhood, in the security of his past life. This explains my nostalgia for the* 'hara' *and* [my use of it] *as a source for* Harafish … [2]

During Mahfouz's childhood the *hara* was very different from what it is today. Today a *hara* or back street in Jamaliyya or elsewhere in Cairo is exclusively inhabited by the lower classes. During the author's childhood, however, the *hara* was in a sense a model of Egyptian society. He tells us that in those days all the classes of the Egyptian people were represented in it, from the very rich to the very poor, and that blocks of flats where whole families lived in single rooms with common facilities stood in close proximity to majestic mansions surrounded by gardens. This strange composition of the *hara* (which according to Mahfouz survived until the 1930s)[3] can explain his frequent use of it as a comprehensive model of society and indeed of humanity at large in *Children of the Alley* and many later works.

One of the main features of the *hara* as Mahfouz knew it in his boyhood was the *futuwwa*, a character type that was later to play a major symbolic role in his fiction, notably *Children of the Alley* and *Harafish.* In his memoirs he tells us that in those days every quarter or *hara* had a *futuwwa* and goes on to describe some of the great battles of the warring gangs to which he was an eyewitness.[4] Elsewhere he defines the part played by the *futuwwa* at the time as not to *oppress the* hara *but to protect it.* Significantly, he goes on to add that *as with some rulers, the protector sometimes turned into a usurper,*[5] and is indeed happy to admit the symbolic part played by the *futuwwas* in his fiction. He argues that in *Children of the Alley, they stood for brutal force*, while in *Harafish* they were more *like rulers, sometimes just, sometimes oppressive.*[6]

Another feature of the *hara* which was to figure centrally in his work, especially *Fountain and Tomb* and *Harafish* was the *takiyya*, from the Turkish *tekke*, a religious foundation of a quasi-monastic type. He refers to it briefly in his memoirs: *there was also a* takiyya *inhabited by Persians or Turks whom we used to see from a distance.*[7] Those mysterious strangers with their enigmatic songs made an impression on the budding consciousness of the author which apparently continued to haunt him until it found artistic expression much later in his life in the works mentioned above.

Mahfouz's childhood observations and experiences in Jamaliyya were not, however, confined to the local scene, for in 1919 when the author was only seven years old, the quarter, together with the rest of the country, was engulfed in a popular uprising against the British occupation. It was in those days that the author probably first came to experience the meaning of nationalist feeling. About the events of that period he said: *From a small room on the roof* [of our house] *I used to see the demonstrations of the 1919 revolution. I saw women take part in the demonstrations on donkey-drawn carts. I often saw English soldiers firing at the demonstrators. My mother used to pull me back from the window, but I wanted to see everything.* From his elementary school opposite the al-Husayn Mosque, he was able, he tells us, to see the bodies of the dead and the wounded laid on the ground: *you could say that the one thing which most shook the security of my childhood was the 1919 revolution.*[8] There is no exaggerating the lasting effect that those public events had on the awareness of the young boy, Mahfouz. For the rest of his life, as his works attest, he was to remain a child of that golden era of the national struggle and a spiritual follower of the liberal, democratic principles of the Wafd Party which inherited the revolution. The events of 1919 are widely recreated and affectionately celebrated in a great many of Mahfouz's novels, notably *The Trilogy.*

Fountain and Tomb, as an autobiographical *Bildungsroman*, is another major work where Mahfouz remembers the 1919 revolution at some length. Tales 12–16, 18–19 and 23 are entirely devoted to the revolution out of a total of 78 episodes in which the more salient memories and impressions of the novelist's early childhood are narrated through the sensibility of a child. All the main events of the revolution from its eruption to the death of its leader, Saad Zaghloul, in 1927 are covered in the tales.

Mirrors is another semi-autobiographical work where ostensibly personal memories of the 1919 events are recalled. Of particular interest here is the episode of 'Anwar al-Halawani' where we can recognise without much difficulty what must have been the real-life origin of the character of Fahmy Abd al-Jawwad in *The Trilogy*. The viewpoint here, like that later used in *Fountain and Tomb*, is that of a child. Here is how he describes the murder of Anwar, the son of a neighbouring family and, like Fahmy, a student at the Law School at the time of the revolution: 'That morning I learnt that our neighbour Anwar al-Halawani had been killed in a demonstration with a bullet fired by an English soldier. Thus I came to know for the first time the meaning of the act of 'murder' in a real-life experience rather than through fairy tales. I also heard for the first time about the 'bullet' as one of the achievements of civilisation. And again there was a new word, 'demonstration' which required a great deal of explanation. It was perhaps also then that I first heard about the representative of a new human race in my little life: the Englishman.'[9]

I have quoted Mahfouz earlier as saying that the events of 1919 could be said to have been what most shook the security of his childhood. A review of the information available on the novelist's childhood (whose source is largely himself) appears to confirm that he grew up in a secure and stable family environment, and his immediate family did not seem to be directly affected by the public dramas of 1919 in any calamitous way. The main sources about the author's childhood are to be found in *The Trilogy* (especially the character of Kamal Abd al-Jawwad) and *Fountain and Tomb*, a fact which the author repeatedly admitted. *Mirrors* is another significant source, though to a lesser extent than the other two. Finally there is his own direct, personal account given in interviews. The author described his childhood in the following terms: *I grew up in a stable family. The atmosphere around me was one which inspired the love of parents and family ... The family was a basic, almost sacred, value of my childhood; I was not one of those who rebelled against their parents or rejected their authority.* The sentiment expressed in this statement is one which was to stay with Mahfouz, taking the form of respect for authority, moderation and a preference for gradual political and social reform, rather than outright revolution – all of which are values which clearly emerge from the totality of the political themes in his work. He tells us that although he was the seventh and last child in a family which already had four boys and two girls, he was virtually deprived of natural sibling relationships. This was, he informs us, because the youngest of his brothers was ten years older than himself.[10] This was not without influence on his fiction: *you can notice that I often portray in my work the relationship between brothers; it is because of my deprivation of it. This is obvious in* The Trilogy, The Beginning and the End *and* Khan al-Khalili.

Mahfouz's description of the family house in which he grew up in Jamaliyya seems largely to tally with that of the house of the Abd al-Jawwad family in *The Trilogy.* He also tells us that the house is associated in his memory with play, particularly on the roof where household provisions were stored, poultry raised and various potted and creeping plants grown. In this connection, readers of such novels as *The Trilogy*, *Khan al-Khalili* and *The Beginning and the End* will recall how the roof figures as an occasional scene for family gatherings and the secret assignations of lovers. Mahfouz also said that, in addition to the roof, he used to play in the street with the children of neighbouring families.[11]

Memories of those young friends and their common street adventures are affectionately recreated in both *Fountain and Tomb* and *Mirrors*.

About his parents Mahfouz does not say much and about his brothers and sisters he says next to nothing. He was at pains, however, to dissociate his parents from the most famous couple of his creation, Ahmad Abd al-Jawwad and Amina of *The Trilogy*. He stressed that the fearful character of Abd al-Jawwad is not modelled on his father, but the head of a neighbouring family in Jamaliyya whom he used to visit as a child with his mother. He described his father as having been *old-fashioned*, but in possession of a gentle temperament. Unlike Abd al-Jawwad, he spent most of his evenings with his family. He used to be some sort of book-keeper or accountant (we are not told exactly what) in the civil service until he took early retirement to manage the business of a merchant friend of his.[12] Mahfouz's account of his father appears, however, to contradict that of Adham Rajab, a lifelong friend of his who knew him well during his adolescent years. Mr Rajab states that the author's father was so strict with his family that the young Mahfouz's friends were never able to visit him at his home. He says that the writer's eldest brother was also strict and surmises that the character of the fierce patriarch Ahmad Abd al-Jawwad in *The Trilogy* must have been based on those two models. When faced with these revelations in 1970, Mahfouz accepted them as true.[13] Surprisingly, however, he was a few years later to contradict himself in the manner explained above.

Mahfouz emphasised that patriotism was one basic value which he picked up from his father in his childhood: *My father always spoke enthusiastically about our national heroes ... I grew up in a home where the names of Mustafa Kamil, Muhammad Farid and Saad Zaghloul were truly sacred ... The strong emotion with which my father spoke about political figures would make you feel as if they were his personal enemies or friends. My father however was no exception here; this was the public spirit which dominated the country during my childhood.*[14] Much of this public spirit and of the infiltration of national politics into the life of the average Egyptian home is immediately recognisable in *The Trilogy.*

Religion was another important value in Mahfouz's family, whereas culture was absent: *You would not have thought that an artist would emerge from that family.*

Mahfouz painfully failed to elaborate on what he calls *the purely religious climate at home*[15] during his childhood. On what it was like and what his response to it was he leaves us totally in the dark. To answer these questions we have to go to Kamal in *The Trilogy* whose gradual disenchantment with religion is described at great length. It is interesting to note here that, while the value of nationalism (in which were also embedded the values of liberalism and democracy) was one that he nurtured and upheld all his life, that of organised, prescribed religion was one which he was to question and finally reject as he reached intellectual maturity.

Of his mother Mahfouz tells us that she was of a *somewhat nervous temperament* and that there was little

Mustafa Kamil (1874–1908) championed the call for ending the British occupation of Egypt. He founded al-Hizb al-Watani (the National Party) in 1907. **Muhammad Farid** (1867–1919) led the National Party after Mustafa Kamil's death in 1908. **Saad Zaghloul** (1860–1927) led Egypt's national struggle for independence from 1918 until his death. His arrest (together with other leaders) and exile by the British authorities in March 1919 triggered the popular revolution of the same year. In 1923 he won the general election and became prime minister. He was idolised as a living symbol of national aspirations. The Wafd (i.e. delegation) Party which he had founded was to remain in the forefront of the national struggle until its abolition after the 1952 coup.

that she shared with the character of Amina in *The Trilogy.* Unlike Amina, and the women of her generation generally, she appears to have enjoyed a considerable amount of freedom. Interestingly, he tells us of her passion for ancient monuments. He remembered that when he was as young as four she would take him to look at the Pyramids and the Sphinx or the Museum of Antiquities, and especially to the Mummies Room. This piece of information is illuminating, considering that the author was later to develop a strong interest in Ancient Egyptian history and that his first three novels were to be devoted to the subject.

Around the year 1924, when Mahfouz was aged 12, the family moved to Abbasiyya, *but I remained attracted to Jamaliyya, always hankering for it*. Mahfouz also tells us that the suburban quarter they moved to in the 1920s was very different from today's over-crowded Abbasiyya: *The Abbasiyya of old times was lush with greenery and had few buildings. Houses were small, consisting only of one storey and each surrounded by a garden, while open fields stretched as far as the horizon ... and the silence was deep.*[16] Next to Jamaliyya, Abbasiyya appears to be the only other place to have made a permanent claim on both Mahfouz's consciousness and his writing. All other Cairene districts that serve occasionally as background for action in his novels are there only in their capacity as realistic detail. The same is also true of his descriptions of Alexandria as in *Autumn Quail*, *The Search*, *The Beggar* and *Miramar*. It is only when he evokes Jamaliyya and Abbasiyya that he seems most at home and that we feel that we are in communion with some part of his innermost soul. Again, it is only evocations of Jamaliyya and Abbasiyya that are employed symbolically in his work to stand for more than their immediate realistic reference. While to Jamaliyya he owes his many recreations of the *hara* with its traditional features, he has the old Abbasiyya lying on the edge of the desert to thank for his evocative descriptions of the *khala'* (open space, emptiness, wasteland, desert). In works like *Children of the Alley* and *Harafish*, to name but two, he brings together the *khala'* of Abbasiyya and the *hara* of Jamaliyya to form his unique Mahfouzland which stands for all the world and all history. In this personalised world-picture, *khala'* is the scene for murders and clandestine burials, and bloody warfare among rival gangs – it is the scene where some of the wildest human passions are set and where the inner loneliness is enhanced by the emptiness outside. But paradoxically, *khala'* is also a place of refuge from the brutality of the world, of soul-searching, of communion with the vast and mysterious universe above, and of visions of goodness and reform. To Abbasiyya and the many friends he made there during his adolescence he is also indebted for a great number of the 55 character vignettes that constitute *Mirrors*. In his old age, the novelist's nostalgia for the Abbasiyya that is now extinct, the youthful days that are now in the distant past and the human relationships that time or death has severed appears to grow ever more agonising – an agony that he gave expression to in his very last novel, *Qushtumur Café* (1988) and in a powerful short story entitled 'Half a Day',[17] both of which are pained attempts at capturing again through feats of memory times and places past.

But above all Mahfouz owes to Abbasiyya one of the most powerful and mystifying experiences of his life which was to be recreated with corresponding intensity in the story of Kamal's unrequited love for Aïda Shaddad in *The Trilogy*. The germination of this key experience in the novel was apparently a quite brief and uneventful encounter in Mahfouz's early youth, but one which in an inscrutable, almost mystical, way had a strong hold on the author's consciousness for the rest of his life. In his memoirs he tries to rationalise the experience in the following terms: *In Abbasiyya I experienced true love for the first time. It was an abstract relationship because of age and class differences. There was actually no communication whatsoever. Had this happened, the experience would perhaps have not acquired much of* [the halo] *that I bequeathed on it. The effects of this relationship were later to appear in the experience of Kamal Abd al-Jawwad's love for Aïda Shaddad in* The Trilogy.[18]

Mahfouz's rendering of this personal experience in *The Trilogy* was not, however, his first. His attempts at domesticating this wildly painful experience into art go as far back as the 1940s. I refer here to a short story entitled 'A Moment's Dream' included in the writer's first collection.[19] The story is structurally weak, but the circumstantial evidence in it leaves us with no doubt that it probably was the author's earliest attempt at achieving catharsis through art. The story is an account of a fleeting encounter between a young scientist and a beautiful young woman – an encounter that consisted in nothing more than the exchange of glances, but one which left the protagonist desperately and obsessively in love and without hope of fulfilment.

Even after the later, more mature and complex rendition of the experience in *The Trilogy*, Mahfouz's feelings still apparently needed further purgation, for he comes back to the subject in the episode entitled 'Safa' al-Katib' in *Mirrors*. This episode, written when he was nearly 60 years old and more than 40 years removed from the experience, shows him still haunted by it and still unable to explain it. Written in intense, poetic language, the account must, however, be seen as the most factual and least fictionalised of his renderings of this key experience of his life. He often described the encounter in near-mystical terms: 'As soon as my eyes caught sight of the girl's face, I embraced one of life's bursting secrets. And again: I saw her in the carriage for a few seconds no more but that was enough for me to lose all willpower and to find myself flung in a

I watched the cart carrying the enchantress of Crimson Lane coming, and drawing it was a winged stallion. I got in and sat at the rear. The steed responded by spreading its wings, and the cart began to fly until we were higher than the rooftops and the minarets – and in seconds we arrived at the Great Pyramid's pinnacle. We started to pass over it from an arm's height above it. But then I rashly leapt down onto the Pyramid's summit, my eyes never departing from the seductive girl as she soared upward and upward – and the night descended, the darkness ever deepening, until she was fixed in the heavens as a luminous star.

'Dream 83' from *The Dreams*

new phase of evolution … I knew how a man could wander away while being there and be wide awake in his sleep, how he could be lost in solitude amidst the crowd and make a companion of pain. I [also knew] how a man could penetrate to the roots of plants and the waves of light.' The episode ends with the narrator in his old age wondering what had become of his love. His words echo with a pain that has not quite subsided: 'Whatever might have become of her and whatever others might have thought of her, did she not have the right to know that she had been worshipped like a goddess in a temple? And that she had once unleashed in a certain heart a life that still throbbed from time to time with her memory?'[20] His heart indeed continued to throb with her memory and crave her as the unattained ideal, inspiring some of his most poetic and eerie writings in his nineties.

The shaping of an intellect

Mahfouz's education, in common with his generation, began at the *kuttab* (Koran school) where he learnt religion and the basics of literacy before he joined the primary school.[21] He recalls briefly his experience at the *kuttab* in *Fountain and Tomb*, but rather than telling us about the educational system, he seems more interested in tracing the beginnings of his nascent sexuality through describing his feelings towards one of the girls there.[22] (In fact, the evolution of the young protagonist's sexuality is a central theme in the book.)[23] About Mahfouz's primary and secondary school education, however, we face a dearth of information concerning the process and its effects on him. Apart from two anecdotal episodes in *Fountain and Tomb* (Tales 21 and 22) and a substantial number in *Mirrors* of sketches of schoolfriends and teachers, and recollections of sit-ins and anti-government demonstrations during the 1920s, there is not much else to know. Significant additional enlightenment, however, can be obtained from the author's account of Kamal's childhood and adolescence in *The Trilogy* (Parts I and II).

In *Fountain and Tomb* the author tells us how he discovered 'reading' at the primary school when a friend lent him a detective story to read. From that time on he became addicted to reading.[24] During the primary stage and the early years of secondary education he moved on from detective stories to historical and adventure novels, all read in translation. He mentions the names of Sir Walter Scott (1771–1832) and Sir Henry Rider Haggard (1856–1925) in this connection. He started writing during school holidays while he was still at the primary school. His method was to rewrite a novel he had read, adding in some details from his own life. As he advanced through his teens he discovered Mustafa Lutfi al-Manfaluti (1876–1924), the Egyptian sentimentalist whose prose style influenced whole generations of educated Egyptians during the early decades of the last century.[25] After Manfaluti comes what he termed *the period of the awakening*. During that period he came to read what he called *the innovators*. Among these he lists the names of Taha Husayn (1889–1973), Abbas Mahmud al-Aqqad (1889–1964), Salama Musa (1888–1958), Ibrahim al-Mazini (1889–1949), Muhammad Husayn Haykal (1888–1956), and (at a slightly later stage) Mahmud Taymur (1894–1973), Tawfiq al-Hakim (1898–1987) and Yahya Haqqi (1905–92). He admitted his indebtedness to these writers for his *emancipation from the traditional way of thinking ... the attraction of* [his] *attention to world literature,* [providing] *a new outlook on classical Arabic literature*, as well as offering him models of the short story, the novel and drama.[26] Taha Husayn's famous book *Fi al-shi'r al-jahili* ('On Pre-Islamic Poetry') (1926), which questioned the validity of received opinion on both the sacred texts of Islam and the secular literature of the period, thereby causing a literary and political uproar at the time, is described by Mahfouz as the book that had the greatest influence on his intellectual development. To him the book was *an intellectual revolution which elevated reason, giving it priority above tradition*.[27] The enthusiasm with which Mahfouz spoke about this book should come as no surprise, as his own work was later to reveal a strong rationalist sense, consistently 'elevating reason above tradition'.

Apart from Taha Husayn, there were two other Egyptian writers whose ideas appear to have influenced the intellect of Mahfouz during its formative years. The first was Salama Musa whose secularist, socialist and evolutionist outlook on life can be found in almost every book that Mahfouz wrote during more than 70 years of his creative life, and whose passion for Ancient (as opposed to Islamic) Egypt can be traced in the novelist's early Pharaonic short stories and novels. Some of Mahfouz's very early writings were printed during the 1930s in *al-Majalla al-jadida* ('The New Review') published by Salama Musa. Also published by Musa was Mahfouz's first novel, *Khufu's Wisdom*, and prior to that his translation from English of a book on Ancient Egypt. In his memoirs Mahfouz recalls his brief personal acquaintance with Musa during his undergraduate years[28] and recreates their encounter in Chapter 13 of *The Trilogy* III, relegating his own part to Ahmad Shawkat rather than Kamal (his usual persona in the novel) and changing the title of the magazine published by Musa to *al-Insan al-jadid* ('The New Human Being'). Elsewhere, Mahfouz admitted: *From Salama Musa I have learnt to believe in science, socialism and tolerance.*[29]

Taha Husayn (1889–1973) was arguably the most original, radical and influential figure of the Arab renaissance of the 20th century. Born in a remote Upper-Egyptian village, blinded by untreated trachoma at the age of five, traditionally taught at the Koran school of his village, then at the Azhar mosque university in Cairo, he nevertheless proceeded to study first at the nascent secular University of Cairo, then at Montpellier and the Sorbonne in France. He approached the study of Islam and Arabic literature from a controversial, secularist, positivist standpoint and argued that Egypt was part of European Mediterranean civilisation in his *The Future of Culture in Egypt* (1938).

The second writer was Abbas Mahmud al-Aqqad whose enquiries into the principles of aestheticism and other philo-

The young Naguib Mahfouz

sophical issues appear to have helped push Mahfouz in the direction of selecting philosophy as the subject to study for his first degree. He tells us that during his secondary education he excelled in mathematics and the sciences and that the assumption had always been that at university he was going to study either medicine or engineering. That was until he started reading the philosophical articles by Aqqad and others, then: *Philosophical questions began to stir deep inside me ... and I imagined that by studying philosophy I would find the right answers for the questions which tormented me ... that I would unravel the mysteries of existence and man's fate.* Thus he joined King Fu'ad I University (now Cairo University) as a philosophy student in 1930–4. The agony which his final choice caused to his father is briefly recalled in Mahfouz's memoirs[30] and unforgettably recreated, with some changes, in the famous scene involving Kamal and his father in Chapter 4 of *The Trilogy* II.

During his secondary school years he also started reading masters of classical Arabic literature. He mentions how he used to imitate their style in his compositions at school, much to the delight of his 'turbanned' Arabic teachers. The effect of these classical readings has in fact survived his school days and can be observed in the propensity in his early short stories and novels towards cliché and flowery outdated style. More positively, the effect of this early (and thenceforth *intermittent*, as he put it) contact with classical Arabic was to endow his Arabic style throughout his career with a purity of phrase and a correctness of grammar and structure which evaded many later writers. He tells us that as he matured he turned more towards classical poetry and mentions in particular the names of the great Abbasid poets, al-Ma'arri (973–1057), al-Mutanabbi (915–65) and Ibn al-Rumi (835–96).[31] It must have been much later that he indulged in reading Sufi (mystical) poetry, the effects of which can be spotted in his fiction from the 1960s onwards. In a later interview he indeed gave the names of Persian poet Hafiz of Shiraz (1320?–92?) and the Bengali poet Rabindranath Tagore (1861–1941) as his two favourite poets.[32]

After graduation in 1934, Mahfouz's intensive readings in philosophy continued as he started working towards an MA degree. His chosen subject, according to one terse statement, was *the aesthetic theory*.[33] Elsewhere, however, he contradicts himself and gives the subject as *Sufism in Islam*.[34] His intellectual interaction with his philosophical studies was recorded in a number of articles that he published in a variety of magazines and newspapers throughout his undergraduate years and for several years thereafter. Mahfouz regarded those articles (most of them written when he was in his early to mid-twenties) as juvenilia and refused to have them collected and republished, which remains the case to date, although a few of them can be found online at his publisher Dar El Shorouk's website (shorouk.com). Thanks to the effort of one scholar, however, we have a full bibliographical list of those early articles, a classification of their content, as well as an attempt at analysing them for the roots of the author's thought.[35]

The list comprises 47 articles written between 1930 and 1945, well over half of which deal with philosophical and psychological subjects. The Mahfouzian scholar Professor Badr points out the prominent place that the thought of the French philosopher Henri Bergson (1859–1941) occupies in those articles, and expounds briefly Bergson's ideas on the duality of body and spirit and his elevation of intuition over scientific reasoning as a way of knowing, arguing that these ideas are necessary for the understanding of Mahfouz's work.[36] One can indeed think of many substantiations in Mahfouz's fiction of the duality of matter and spirit and man's struggle to evolve from the bonds of the first to the freedom of the latter (the schism of Saber, the protagonist of *The Search*, between his two lovers is perhaps the most clear-cut example in Mahfouz's *oeuvre*.)

Bergson's influence on Mahfouz was indeed tremendous and far exceeded Badr's suggestions. The philosopher's most telling impact on Mahfouz's thought was probably in the sphere of his ideas on time and memory. Bergson's notion of 'duration', of time as a continuum, a perpetual flux (as distinguished from the spatialised, measurable conception of time), lies at the very foundation of *The Trilogy*. There is little doubt either that Mahfouz's concept of time as 'representing the evolutionary spirit of man',[37] central again to *The Trilogy* and probably the only source of philosophical optimism in the author's entire corpus, was drawn from Bergson's notion of 'creative evolution'. Nor was Mahfouz's fascination with Bergson's thought a transient one. Far from being limited to *The Trilogy*, it is to be found also in *Children of the Alley*, *Harafish* and *Arabian Nights and Days*; in other words, in all those works which portray the evolutionary flux of history and the perpetual tug-of-war between the forces of moral progress and those of the baser instincts. On the individual (as opposed to collective) level, Mahfouz's obsession with the dichotomy between the unity and perpetuity of mnemonic time and the discreteness and transience of spatialised time (such as we see in *Qushtumur Café* and the short story 'Half a Day', discussed later) was yet another manifestation of the enormous power of Bergson's influence on him. In respect of notions of time, Bergson's influence on Mahfouz was indeed reinforced by that of Marcel Proust (1871–1922), whose own *A la recherche du temps perdu* (published 1913–27) (much admired by Mahfouz) was itself influenced by Bergson's ideas.

Another Bergsonian notion active in Mahfouz's creations is perhaps that of the 'two moralities'. Bergson defines two sources for morality, one based on 'intelligence' and the other on 'intuition'. It is the second one which concerns us here since it finds 'its expression not only in the creativity of art and philosophy but also in the mystical experience of the saints'.[38] The mystical (or Sufi) experience was a key one in Mahfouz's work from Radwan Hussainy in *Midaq Alley* to Ali al-Junaydi in *The Thief and the Dogs*, Omar al-Hamzawi in *The Beggar*, and Abdullah al-Balkhi in *Arabian*

Nights and Days. Mahfouz's attitude to his mystics is, however, ambivalent, for while they are shown as humans with an impeccable superior morality, their 'sainthood' is depicted as a personal achievement of little relevance to society, as will be shown later. Suffice it to say here that of all Bergson's notions, it is this last one that Mahfouz appears to embody in his work only in order to reject it.

Mahfouz's MA in philosophy was never to happen, and within two years of graduation his orientation towards philosophy was deflected in the direction of literature. Thus a harrowing conflict in Mahfouz's mind between philosophy and literature which had lasted for the period of those two years was brought to an end in favour of the latter.[39] Mahfouz's inner conflict is externalised in *The Trilogy* III through the lengthy dialogues between Kamal and his friend Riyad Qaldas, with Kamal arguing the case for philosophy and Riyad that for art.

Having decided to abandon the study of philosophy, Mahfouz had much to catch up with. He drew on a general guide to world literature, namely *The Outline of Literature* by John Drinkwater, to help him in planning his reading and selecting material.[40] The book's method consisted in reviewing world literature down the ages and across nations, which afforded Mahfouz an overall view rather than immersing him in the literature of any single period or nation. Because he started late, as he put it, he had to be selective, confining himself to the main figures, and then only to their best-known masterpieces. He also began with the modern period, occasionally going back to earlier periods. His medium was English and, to a much lesser extent, French: he read Proust in English, but Anatole France (1844–1924) in the original. Later in his life he came to depend on Arabic translations as they began to be more common.

Over and over again Mahfouz gave his interviewers an account of the writers he admired and the works which most impressed him. His list is long and varied and is proof of an overriding orientation towards Western culture. I shall quote one of his accounts at length. His comments on writers and works are fascinating in their uninhibited spontaneity. Often, however, they are revealing about his own inclinations and writings: *The writers who influenced me are the ones I liked. I liked Tolstoy and Dostoevsky, Chekhov and Maupassant ... Of modernist writers I liked Proust and Kafka. As for Joyce ... he was just a writer that you had to read ...* Ulysses *was a terrible novel, but it created a trend ... In the theatre I liked Shakespeare immensely ... Both his grandness and ironies entered my soul and made me feel at home with him ... Next to Shakespeare I liked Eugene O'Neill much and also Ibsen and Strindberg. In the contemporary theatre I was truly shaken by Beckett's* Waiting for Godot. *As for Chekhov's theatre, I found it flaccid and boring. In American literature I rate Melville's* Moby Dick *among the world's greatest novels if not the greatest. Out of Hemingway's work I only liked* The Old Man and the Sea. *His other work left me surprised at the fame he has acquired. I did not like Faulkner; he is too complicated. I also liked Dos Passos, but none of them has written a* Moby Dick. *I very much admire the all-encompassing outlook in Conrad's* Heart of Darkness. *The novel offers a very realistic story but contains at the same time a broad universal view. This is what I have been trying to do in my latest novels* [NB interview was given in 1973].

As for the latest trends, the Angry Young Men etc, you could say that their influence has not gone beyond the surface of my skin. 'Le roman nouveau' is rubbish. It is as if you were saying, 'life is boring therefore I will write for you an equally boring novel'. The fact is that any expression of the boredom of life must be entertaining ... In poetry I was fascinated by Shakespeare, Tagore and Hafiz of Shiraz; they are the closest poets to my soul.[41]

Elsewhere he informs us that he owes his training in the realistic tradition to its later developers rather than early masters: *I got to know realism through contemporary writers like Galsworthy, Aldous Huxley and D H Lawrence. After these I was no longer able to read Dickens. Nor was I able to read Balzac having already read Flaubert and Stendhal.*[42] To the Russian masters mentioned above he adds the name of Gorky, but deems him of a lower rank. His fiction, he argues, is parochial and too dependent on the message it contains.

Asked in yet another interview about the Western writers who most influenced him he listed three names as his first choice: Tolstoy, Proust and Thomas Mann. He regretted that since reading *War and Peace* and *A la recherche du temps perdu* early on in his life he never had the time to go back to them again. His fascination with *War and Peace* is understandable in the context of his own authorship of another great novel dealing with the effect of social and political upheaval on the lives of individuals, i.e. *The Trilogy.* It is worth noting here that Mahfouz does not give another famous saga novel, viz. John Galsworthy's (1867–1933) *Forsyte Saga* (published 1906–21 and thought by many commentators to have been an influence on his own *Trilogy*) any special rank as a great novel. He lists Galsworthy, however, among the authors he read. Equally interesting is Mahfouz's dismissal of Charles Dickens as an author he could not read in spite of the affinity observed by many critics between a novel like *Midaq Alley* and the typical Dickensian world. On the other hand, we can understand his fascination with Proust's *A la recherche du temps perdu* in the light of his own unrelenting obsession with the theme of observable time versus time in memory. If one is to see a pattern in Mahfouz's comments on writers from whom he learnt his profession, we may be able to say that he, perhaps subconsciously, tends to play down the influence of those whose achievement has been equalled or surpassed in his own work, while he continues to hold in charmed esteem those, like Tolstoy and Proust, whose attainments are deemed unsurpassable.

Mahfouz often repeated that when he started writing his realistic novels in the 1940s he was well aware that realism was already a spent force in Europe and that he had already read Proust, Joyce, Lawrence and other contemporary modernists. However, when it came to writing, he argued, he felt that since the novel was still a nascent form in Arabic without an established tradition in realism, he could not move straight away from romanticism to modernism: the Arabic novel and his own experience as a novelist in the making had to go through the natural stages of evolution. This contention of Mahfouz's can withstand enquiry. We can indeed see modernist influences in the heart of his realistic phase, such as the occasional use of the stream of consciousness technique and his early experiment with the psychological novel in *The Mirage*. Another piece of evidence that supports this contention is the fact that the moment Mahfouz felt that he had mastered the techniques of realism and exhausted their potential by writing *The Trilogy*, he was to cast realism behind him and plunge into the deep and turbulent waters of modernism.

While the earliest examples of the novel as a genre in English, for instance, can be traced back to the 17th century, it entered Arabic literature, rich in its own old narrative traditions, in the 19th century through translations from European languages. The earliest Arabic novels go back only to the 1870s, with more accomplished works coming decades later. The Arabic novel was still a 'child' when Mahfouz started writing. It fell to him to bring it up.

One of the inconsistencies, however, in Mahfouz's comments on his work is his persistent denial of the influence of the naturalist school on the realistic phase of his corpus of work. The persistence of his denial was in fact a reaction to an equally persistent and unanimous recognition by his critics of this influence in his work. Critics often cite the characters of Nefisa from *The Beginning and the End* and Yasin from *The Trilogy* (a list which can certainly be expanded) as salient examples. Mahfouz, on the other hand, admitted reading much of Emile Zola (1840–1902) and his followers, but insisted that in his work 'heredity' is of no consequence and that it is the effect of 'environment' that reigns supreme. However, he seems to contradict himself when he argued in the same breath that Nefisa's poverty (environment) in addition to her ugliness (heredity) helped shape her life. Elsewhere he proclaimed that all considerations, social, psychological and *biological* (my italics), influence his characters.[43] Mahfouz's denial of naturalistic influence on his work cannot therefore withstand the testimony of his own fiction nor, for that matter, his own conflicting statements on the subject. His attempt at denying this influence stemmed, I believe, from a concern that stressing the hereditary connection in his fiction might result in overshadowing the supreme importance of social and political conditions in shaping human behaviour, a belief that lies at the heart of his work. Another significant element here is the fact that all these denials of naturalism were made by Mahfouz at a time when he had moved out of his realistic phase and when heredity had in fact stopped playing any role in his fiction. It was as if, having outgrown a particular concept, he wanted to go back and obliterate it from his literary past.

Two influences which Mahfouz was, however, happy to admit were those of James Joyce (1882–1941) in his use of the internal monologue on the one hand, and surrealism and the theatre of the absurd (both whose influence can be spotted in some of his short stories and one-act plays written in the aftermath of the Arab defeat in the 1967 war with Israel) on the other hand. He insisted, however, that blind imitation had never been the case with him; that all the techniques he borrowed were modified to suit his purposes and clearly stamped with his own artistic insignia. With regard to his use of the internal monologue he had this to say: *The internal monologue is a method, a vision and a way of life; and even though I use it, you cannot say that I belong to its school as such. All that happens is that I sometimes encounter a Joycean moment in my hero's life, so I render it in Joyce's manner with some modification.*[44]

He also played down the influence of the theatre of the absurd on his work. He argued that the absurd outlook on life maintains that it is meaningless, whereas for him life has a meaning and a purpose, and that though his work might have given in to an absurd moment in his own or his nation's life, his was a sense of absurdity that was *rationalised, explicable and subdued*, unlike the European brand, which was total and absolute.[45] Mahfouz summed it all up in connection with the question of influence when he proclaimed: *I have not come out of the cloak of any one writer, nor can I be stood under the banner of any one technique.*[46]

On the question of the influence of earlier Egyptian novelists, Mahfouz was again conservative, if not dismissive. With the exception of Jurji Zaydan (1861–1914), he made no mention of Syrian pioneers like Salim al-Bustani (1846–84) and Fransis al-Marrash (1836–73). Of Tawfiq al-Hakim's (1898–1987) *'Awdat al-ruh* ('The Return of the Spirit') (1933), he said that he found it more akin to drama than to fiction. Taha Husayn and Abbas al-Aqqad, he maintained, were 'thinkers' whose concern with the novel was only secondary. He admitted, however, that Taha Husayn's novel *Shajarat al-bu's* (1944), translated as *The Tree of Misery* (Palm Press, Cairo: 1997), was instrumental in focusing his attention on writing a saga novel. It was after reading it, he tells us, that he went on to read more of the same, namely Galsworthy's *The Forsyte Saga*, Tolstoy's *War and Peace* and Thomas Mann's (1875–1955) *Buddenbrooks* (1900) before he wrote his own *Trilogy.*[47] Asked on one occasion to clarify a statement he had made earlier in which he said that he had been influenced by the Egyptian novelists Ibrahim al-Mazini (1890–1949) and Yahya Haqqi (1905–92), he gave this rather loose definition of influence: *When I say that I was influenced* [by a certain writer] *what I mean is that I liked* [his work]. *My assumption is that I am influenced by the writers I like.*[48] His attitude towards the question of influence on himself by earlier Arab novelists is eloquently summed up in his pronouncement: *There was no legacy of the novel* [in Arabic] *that I could depend on …*

I arrived on a scene that was nearly empty. It was incumbent on me to discover things and to lay the ground by myself.[49]

Finally, no review of the intellectual influences that helped shape the thought and art of Mahfouz is complete without mention of science. Belief in science, in conjunction with socialism, as a major force in shaping modern society and the future of mankind is at the centre of the novelist's work. His preoccupation with science was demonstrated as early as his first two realistic novels, *Khan al-Khalili* and *Cairo Modern*, to reach a climax in *Children of the Alley*, where science is shown to inherit the traditional role of religion in reforming human society. His readings in science for the layman went back to his early youth. He mentioned such subjects as biology, physics, anthropology and the origin of matter, and admitted that his readings in science had a tremendous effect on his thinking.[50]

Mahfouz, as we have seen, was careful to fight off any suggestion of influence in the sense of imitation, especially in connection with Western writers and literary schools. He was nevertheless happy to articulate his admiration for European culture and his belief in the inevitability of the triumph of its values. He was also at pains to establish a historic affinity between it and Arab culture. His views in this respect are indeed reminiscent of those expressed earlier by Taha Husayn in his controversial book, *The Future of Culture in Egypt*, published in 1938.[51] Mahfouz argued that: *Our culture is very close to European culture. This is because they both are based on common foundations. For its part, European culture is based on both the moral principles of the Bible and the modern science inherited from the Greeks. The same is also true of Arabic culture, the difference between the Bible and the Koran being here of no consequence as the latter maintains that it embraces both the Bible and the Gospels. The moral values are thus the same. As for the Greeks, we know that the Arabs translated the Greeks and studied them ... Both our culture and that of the West belong in fact to one family.* Again in a reference to

European culture in the context of a discussion of the permanently hot issue of foreign influence and cultural identity, he announced unequivocally: *I believe that there is no escape from the supremacy of the more efficient culture, and this can only be for the good of mankind.*[52] These relatively late and explicit views have their testimony in the totality of Mahfouz's work, where the traditional values of modern Europe such as secularism, social liberalism, parliamentary democracy, socialism and belief in science are glorified.

In his later years, however, the author's intellectual stance *vis-à-vis* this question seems to have shifted somewhat. In an interview given in 1987, he argued that in the past he used to believe that modern (European) civilisation was the only viable one by dint of its being an assimilation of all past civilisations – Egyptian, Mesopotamian, Greek, Roman and Arab; and that as such it ought to be the universal civilisation of mankind. More recently, he went on to say, he came to believe that different civilisations upheld essentially different worldviews. He felt this caused his enthusiasm for Western civilisation to shift towards an enthusiasm for a universal human need such as science, which in turn can be used in the service of the worldview of one's own culture. Mahfouz concluded by describing his present position as an eclectic one which sought to benefit from the entire human legacy.[53] This shift in his thinking remains, however, at the theoretical level. It probably came too late in his life to be able to be substantiated in his work. One may argue nevertheless that his movement in the last three decades or so of his life away from the European mould of the novel towards a more indigenously inspired form was a mark of his waning fascination with all things Western, but one would have to make the reservation here that the divergence was more in form than substance.

Politics, religion and society
Politics was a major concern of Mahfouz throughout his creative

Mahfouz, lower left, with sunglasses, in a demonstration for Egyptian–
Syrian unity

career, a fact he himself emphasises: *In all my writing, you will find politics. You may find a story which ignores love, or any other subject, but not politics; it is the very axis of our thinking.*[54] Highly politicised in his thinking and writing though he was, he was never politically active in the formal sense of joining a political party or occupying political office under any of the many regimes that his life spanned. His political awareness started blossoming, as we have seen, at the rather early age of seven with the eruption of the 1919 revolution. This awareness must have matured during his high school and university years in the late 1920s and early 1930s. The national struggle during that period had two objectives which were closely related, namely independence from the British and the estab-lishment of true democratic government in the face of absolutist monarchism. During the years up to the 1952 coup led by Jamal Abd al-Nasir (Nasser) (1918–70), this national struggle was led by the Wafd Party which had arisen from the ashes of 1919. The Wafd was, by and large, the conscience of the nation and the focus of its political hopes. Mahfouz evinced great sympathy for the party and its leaders in his novels dealing with that period (especially *The Trilogy*). His sympathy for the Wafd, however, never took official form. According to him, he only participated as an individual in *general popular actions like demonstrations and strikes ... no matter how dangerous these were.*[55]

Another political movement active at the time was socialism, whose ideas were attractive to intellectuals although it lacked both a popular base and a recognised political organ. It cannot be doubted that socialist ideals must have claimed Mahfouz's soul from very early on in his youth. The influence of socialist thought figures strongly in his first two social novels (*Khan al-Khalili* and *Cairo Modern*) and continued ever afterwards. Parallel to this sympathy for socialism was an antipathy towards

Jamal Abd al-Nasir (Nasser) (1918–70) led the Free Officers' movement in the Egyptian army who staged a coup in 1952, ending almost 150 years of the rule of the Muhammad Ali dynasty and turning Egypt into a republic. His rule brought major social, political and economic changes to Egypt, adopting socialist, state-controlled policies aiming at achieving social justice, but creating a totalitarian regime in the process. His defiance of the former colonial powers over the nationalisation of the Suez Canal in 1956 won him widespread popularity in the Arab world and encouraged his pan-Arabist policies leading to full unity with Syria in 1958, but this collapsed three years later. Defeat by Israel in the Six-Day War of 1967 was a major blow, leading to his temporary resignation. He died of a heart attack in 1970.

Islamic fundamentalism as expressed by the Muslim Brotherhood, a considerable political force in the 1930s and 1940s with strong organisation and a not-insignificant power base among the people. Unlike socialism, which is idealised in Mahfouz's work, Islamism is rejected as unsuitable for modern times. Mahfouz's distaste for religious fundamentalism never waned with time. In his memoirs he does not mince his words when he proclaims in the course of reviewing political forces active on the scene during his youth: *the ones I hated from the beginning were the Muslim Brothers.*[56] In his semi-autobiographical work, *Mirrors*, he draws a very negative portrait of a prominent leader of the movement, viz. Sayyid Qutb (1906–66),[57] whom he knew personally in his youth at a time when Qutb had shown more interest in literary criticism than in active religious fundamentalism (Qutb was in fact among the first critics to draw attention to the budding talent of Mahfouz in the mid-1940s).

It must, however, be emphasised that in spite of Mahfouz's firm belief in socialism as the only way forward for his society, he cannot be pigeonholed as a Marxist in any tight definition of the word. He asserted that he did not consider himself a Marxist despite his immense sympathy for Marxism. He admitted that he had his doubts about the Marxist theory as a philosophical system, but went on to list aspects of Marxism which he would like to see applied in human society. His words amount to a political credo.

I believe:

1 *that man should be freed from the class system and what it entails of privileges such as inheritance ... etc;*

2 *that man should be freed from all forms of exploitation;*

3 *that an individual's position* [in society] *should be determined according to both his natural and acquired qualifications;*

4 *that recompense should be equal to need;*

5 *that the individual should enjoy freedom of thought and belief under protection of law to which both governor and governed should be subject;*

6 *in the realisation of democracy in the fullest sense;*

7 *in the reduction of the power of central government so that it should be restricted to* [internal?] *security and defence.*[58]

Central to the understanding of the bulk of Mahfouz's work from the beginning of the 1960s to the end of his life is an adequate grasp of his attitude to the 1952 revolution, a subject on which he had spoken outside the scope of his fiction with a profuseness which was only paralleled by his extensive preoccupation with it in his creative writing. The year 1952, when Mahfouz had completed the writing of *The Trilogy*,[59] heralded an uncharacteristic stalemate in his creative life: he was to stop writing until 1957, when he started work on *Children of the Alley*. By way of explaining this stalemate, he argued that he felt that the society he had been writing about for years had changed overnight and that many of the social ills which had moved him to write were remedied by the new regime.[60] There is no reason to doubt the truthfulness of this remark in so far as it applied to the early years of the revolution, but as the years went by and the shortcomings of the Nasser era began to make themselves felt, one critic's remark that Mahfouz, 'rather than finding nothing to say ... was unable to say what he wanted to' rings true.[61] This seems even more the case when we look at the content of what the novelist began to say when he had recovered. His first novel after the silent period, viz. *Children of the Alley*, was an allegorical lamentation of the failure of mankind to achieve social justice and to harness the potential of science in the service of mankind, rather than its destruction. Masked in allegory though it was, the novel could hardly be seen as the offspring of an intellect basking in a sense of revolutionary fulfilment. The publication of his next novel, *The Thief and the Dogs* in 1961, shows in unequivocal terms that his disillusionment with the revolution was complete. Almost all the novels of the 1960s can in fact be seen as a barrage of bitter criticism aimed at a revolution that has abjectly failed to deliver the goods.

It must be stressed, however, that Mahfouz's quarrel with the 1952 revolution was never over its principles; it was rather over practices which failed to live up to them. He proclaimed in an interview given in the relatively freer climate of 1973 (three years into the era of Anwar al-Sadat (1918–81)): *There is no doubt that the declared aims of the 23 July* [1952] *revolution would have been to me and to my entire generation very satisfactory only if they had been carried out in the spirit in which they were declared ... I wanted nothing more than true socialism and true democracy. This has not been achieved.*[62] Following the military debacle of 1967 and Nasser's death in 1970, Mahfouz's onslaught on the revolution rose to a crescendo in *Karnak Café* (1974), a bitter condemnation of the repressive rule of the police state and its destruction of the dignity of the individual and hence the nation as a whole.

The novelist's ambivalent attitude towards the 1952 revolution can perhaps be best illustrated by two separate passages from *Mirrors.* Here is the first passage (from the sketch titled 'Adli al-Muadhin') in which the narrator/protagonist of the novel (a persona for Mahfouz) expresses his early enthusiasm for the revolution: *I felt for the first time in my life that a wave of justice was sweeping away without letup the deep-rooted rot and I wished that it would stay on its course without hesitation or aberration, and for ever remaining pure.*[63]

Further on in the book in the sketch entitled 'Qadri Rizq', the narrator draws a portrait of a member of his group of friends who belonged to the Free Officers' Movement which carried out the 1952 coup. The character, obviously meant to be representative of the top echelons of the revolution, is portrayed critically but with unmistakable affection. Here are the closing lines of the episode: 'Qadri Rizq is counted among the sincere and respected men of the revolution. He may be difficult to classify in accordance with universal principles, but he can be described accurately in the light of the Charter.[64] He believes in social justice as much as private ownership and individual incentives, in scientific socialism as much as religion, in nationalism as much as pan-Arabism, in the legacy of the past as much as science, and in a popular base as much as absolute government. Nevertheless, whenever I see him walking in with his limp and his remaining eye, my heart beats with affection and admiration.'[65] The revolution here is ridiculed as a mixture of conflicting social and political principles, while the officer's deformities (dating from the Suez War) are obvious symbols of the revolution's shortcomings. The evident affection is, however, proof of the ambivalence in Mahfouz's attitude towards the rule of Nasser: he consistently showed himself to be equally aware of both the positive and negative sides of the experiment.

Mahfouz, as we have seen, was born into a lower-middle-class Cairene family and his work remained very much the product of this fact. The background for his fiction is always urban: mainly Cairo and occasionally Alexandria; the countryside has no place in his world. His fiction is inhabited by members of his own class; their progress within society, their loves and hates, ambitions and frustrations, both private and public, are vividly recreated. The aristocracy, the upper middle class, the working class and the peasantry form no part of his customary scene and when individuals from those groups make an occasional appearance in his fiction, they are usually portrayed from outside and through the eyes of the petit-bourgeois protagonist, their importance being drawn solely from their relationship with him (a striking example is to be found in *Miramar* where the peasant heroine Zohra is at the centre of the action, yet the novel is told from four points of view, but not hers).

Thus Mahfouz has been labelled by critics (and perhaps rightly so) as the novelist of the small bourgeoisie.[66] It is a label that he appeared to resent at first, but to which he later became resigned, professing his 'bias' for the small bourgeoisie, which he viewed as *the candidate for the salvation of humanity*. The upper bourgeoisie, he explained, is arrogant and seeks to control and exploit the people. The proletariat, on the other hand, is equally intent on wrenching power from its exploiters. Only the small bourgeoisie with its middle stance between the extreme positions of the classes above and below itself is capable of recognising the advantages and faults of both sides and evolving an order viable for everyone. Mahfouz went on to illustrate his point in interesting, if somewhat eccentric, terms: *A good small bourgeois rejects the shortcomings of the upper bourgeoisie such as exploitation and love of power at the same time as he admires its inclination towards knowledge, art and refinement of manners. On the other hand he is also aware of the vices of the proletariat forced upon them by poverty, but he is equally aware of their genuine mettle and the fact that they represent the majority. No wonder then that the small bourgeoisie produced Socialist Democracy which combines the best in Liberalism and Communism. Such was the case in history too. For religions whose prophets were kings or princes like Akhenatunism and Judaism failed to spread widely, contrary to Christianity and Islam whose prophets belonged to the small bourgeoisie – a carpenter and a small merchant, respectively.*[67]

A life in the civil service

Like many of his characters Mahfouz was a civil servant.[68] From the year of his graduation (1934) to his retirement (1971), he served in a wide variety of government departments in various capacities and under different political regimes. Thus Mahfouz was not able to devote himself entirely to literature until he retired from work at the official age of 60. 'What a waste!' is one's first impulse, but in fact it was quite the opposite. Mahfouz's fiction is profoundly indebted to his civil service career for an infinite variety of types, individuals, plots, settings, images, symbols, atmospheres – he had admirably succeeded in finding a metaphor for the human condition in the drab world of the minor Egyptian civil servant (a notable example is his short novel, *Respected Sir*).

In 1934 he joined the administration of King Fu'ad I University as a clerk (there, for instance, he picked up the model for Ahmad Akif, the eccentric hero of *Khan al-Khalili*). In 1938 he moved to the Ministry of Religious Endowments, where he worked as parliamentary secretary to the minister. The variety of claimants there that he came in contact with in his official capacity ranged, according to him, from descendants of the Ottoman Sultan, Abdulhamid II, to poor Egyptian peasants. Those claimants of *waqf* (revenue from religious endowments) and their stories were later to provide his fiction with a great many characters and situations, most notably the eccentric protagonist of *Heart of the Night.* In 1945 he was transferred to the al-Ghuri Library in Jamaliyya at his own request, thereby returning to his birthplace, which was to remain a permanent spiritual refuge for him and a fathomless source of inspiration for his fiction. His duties at the library appear to have been so light as to allow him, on the one hand, to wander in the area and spend time in its cafés, watching human types and imprinting pictures of places on his memory and, on the other hand, to indulge in major reading projects – it was at that time that he read Proust's *A la recherche du temps perdu* (in English translation). From there he moved on, still in the service of the Ministry of Endowments and still in Jamaliyya, to manage the Good Loan Project, an interest-free loan scheme for the destitute. It was a period of his life that he enjoyed fully: he spent whole mornings chatting with lower-class women who came to apply for loans. But it was not totally idle chatter; many of those women later came to populate his fiction, especially in the realistic phase.

The early 1950s brought Mahfouz's connection with the Endowments to an end and saw him move to the seemingly more appropriate sphere of information and culture. For the next 20 years or so of his civil service career (all under the regime of Nasser's revolution) he was to occupy fairly influential cultural posts: secretary to the Minister of National Guidance; director of the Film Censorship Office; director-general of the Film Support Organisation; adviser to the General Organisation of Film Industry, Broadcasting and Television; chairman of the board of directors of the same; and finally, adviser to the Minister of Culture. When he retired in 1971, he was invited to join *al-Ahram* newspaper, which at that time attracted to its exclusive pages the cream of Egyptian writers in their later years. Most of his fiction from 1959 onwards was serialised in it. He also contributed a short weekly column on topical, mostly non-literary issues from the mid-1970s until his death. It is worth noting that human models drawn from the milieu of the first half of his career mostly populated the corresponding half of his output, i.e. from *Khan al-Khalili* up to *Children of the Alley.* Novels written after that seem to have drawn mainly on the environment of the second half of his career. Here we meet many intellectuals, professionals and high government officials in contrast with the lower and lower-middle classes of his earlier work. However, this division is by no means rigid, for models of the earlier half crossed this imaginary barrier all the time, and increasingly so since the mid-1970s when, with works like *Fountain and Tomb* and *Harafish,* it became apparent that Mahfouz was experiencing nostalgia for his old world.

From the late 1940s and up to the early 1980s Mahfouz also worked as an occasional freelance film screenwriter. Altogether he wrote the scenarios for 25 films, many of which are today counted among the classics of the Egyptian cinema. Significantly though, there are to date at least 40 films and a large number of TV series based on his own work, for which he did not write a single scenario himself: he would not interfere with the adaptation of his own work for the cinema. Though he originally started writing scenarios as a way of supplementing his income, the experience was to have an influence on his literary style, particularly in his use of the montage technique and flashbacks which began to feature noticeably in his work from the 1960s onwards.

Mahfouz was a prolific writer with an output reaching 33 novels (35 if the *Trilogy* is counted as three works), 16 collections of short stories and plays, in addition to a number of miscellaneous works difficult to categorise under traditional genres, such as

Echoes of an Autobiography and *The Dreams* (both consisting mostly of very short, eerie narratives written in highly poetic language), not to mention collected and uncollected journalism and one early translation.[69] Though his first novel was published in 1939, his fame and reputation were to grow slowly and it was not until the publication of *The Trilogy* in 1956–7 that he was hailed as the unrivalled master of fiction in the Arabic tongue. In 1970 he was awarded the State Prize for Literature. Though Mahfouz was first translated into the main languages of the world in the 1960s, interest in him in the West remained largely confined to orientalists and students of Arabic, while publication of translations of his work was mainly in the hands of academic and small-circulation publishers. Nevertheless, by the late 1980s the strength of his reputation among learned circles in the West as a writer with a universal human appeal and a lifetime's achievement was such that he was awarded the Nobel Prize for Literature in 1988, thereby becoming the first Arab writer to win the prize. Translations of his work into English, French and many other languages acquired new momentum after the Nobel award and their publication was undertaken by mainstream commercial publishers. Today more than 25 titles of his are available in English alone.

The man and the artist

Mahfouz remained a bachelor until the age of 43 – for many years he had laboured under the conviction that marriage with its restrictions and commitments would hamper his literary future (compare Kamal's bachelorhood in *The Trilogy* I). His prolonged bachelorhood gave him the opportunity to know many women, all of whom, he tells us, were later to appear in his fiction. In 1954, however, his defences against marriage collapsed when he married Atiyyatallah Ibrahim, who remained largely out of the glare of publicity in which her husband lived. The marriage produced two daughters, Umm Kulthum (named after the famous Egyptian

Mahfouz (centre) with the singer Umm Kulthum (left) and Tawfiq al-Hakim (right)

singer adored by Mahfouz) and Fatima (named after his mother), or Huda and Fatin as they prefer to be called. Mahfouz had always jealously defended his privacy against the curiosity of the media, but the onslaught in the wake of the Nobel Prize in 1988 was too fierce to resist and it was only then that journalists and cameras were admitted to his house and the public were allowed a glimpse of his family life. When he got married he moved from the family house in Abbasiya to a houseboat on the Nile then soon to an apartment also overlooking the Nile in Giza where he lived until his death. It is worth noting that the Nile did not play a major role in his fiction until some time after his move to the neighbourhood near the ancient river. Full recognition of the effect of this change of habitat on his creative imagination of Mahfouz appeared in the 1966 novel, *Adrift on the Nile*, as well as much later works such as *The Day the Leader was Killed* in 1985.

In all his life Mahfouz left Egypt only twice: going once to Yemen[70] and once to Yugoslavia – both visits being on short, official missions. He had very much wished to travel to Europe and study in France in his youth in the manner of Tawfiq al-Hakim and other Egyptian writers, but there was no opportunity. European literature as well as European social and political thought had a tremendous influence on his intellect: it will always be a matter for surmise as to how this influence would have been tempered or, for that matter, enhanced through direct, prolonged contact with Western culture. As he grew older and more established and opportunities became available, he had become too set in his ways, too enslaved by a routine of work and life to care to disrupt it. 'It seems to me that I am naturally inclined to staying put. The idea of travelling

Known affectionately as 'al-Sitt' – the lady – the singer Umm Kulthum (1898–1975) was a country girl whose voice first captivated Cairo audiences under the monarchy. She was initially banned from Egypt's airwaves after the Free Officers took power, but Nasser reversed the decision and she became an icon of the new regime. After Egypt's defeat by Israel in 1967, she withdrew to her villa in Zamalek, but soon changed her mind, throwing herself into a marathon round of concerts to raise money to rebuild Egypt's shattered army. Umm Kulthum became one of Arab nationalism's most enduring cultural symbols. Her funeral in 1975 drew around four million mourners.

alarms me – I mean the trouble and hassle, not the sightseeing and discovery. If only it were possible for the world to parade past while I stood where I am!'[71] This was so much the case that when he was awarded the Nobel Prize in 1988 he refused to travel to receive it in person. Ironically, three years later he was forced to travel to London in the winter of 1991 for heart surgery.

No account of Mahfouz's life can be complete without mention of the *maqha* (café) and the important role it played both in his life and in his fiction. In his youth, in common with men of his generation, the café acted as a social club, much like the pub in

Britain. There personal and literary friendships were forged and many intellectual, heart-searching discussions took place; proof of which we find in the many café scenes involving Kamal in *The Trilogy*, to give but one example. In later years, Mahfouz used the cafés of Cairo (and Alexandria in the summer) as literary salons where he met his literary peers and where scores of young aspiring writers came to listen to him and debate intellectual issues with him. There is hardly a novel by Mahfouz in which the café does not represent a significant part of the scene, and there are several in which the café is the most important element in the setting. Two actually have as their titles the names of the cafés where the action unfolds: *Karnak Café* and *Qushtumur Café*. At least the first of these is known to be closely based on Maqha Orabi,[72] a favourite haunt of Mahfouz in Abbasiyya that has since been demolished.

Critics of Mahfouz agree that he is a skilful literary architect with a great sense for structure and the almost geometric organisation of material. This literary quality was if anything a reflection of his personal temperament, the daily fabric of his life over many decades having been as tightly structured and the details of its pattern as carefully organised as if it had been one of his own novels. In fact, Mahfouz's legendary reputation for self-discipline, ruthless control over his time and total subservience to the force of habit all make a mockery of the conventional image of the artist as a bohemian creature.

Mahfouz habitually sought to alleviate the horror that interviewers confronted him with over this matter by simply explaining it as a by-product of the necessity of combining a civil servant's full-time job with a creative writer's: he had to organise the second half of the day so carefully in order to have the time to read and write. This was even more necessary as a chronic allergy affecting his eyes rendered him incapable of writing from April to the end of the summer, so that he only had the winter months for his creative pursuits. He also made little of what he called *the*

Mahfouz with his wife and daughters

luxury of inspiration and confessed that once an idea was past the thinking stage (which could go on for years, as in the case of *The Trilogy*), nothing would stop him from sitting at his desk for two or three hours every evening until the work was completed. He wrote first drafts quickly and spent a longer time over revision and rewriting. He maintained that the revised text was often substantially different from the first one, though the central idea usually hardly changed.

Rigorously disciplined and readily dismissive of romantic ideas about the creative process though he was, he still happily described his first conception of a work in terms of a *tremor* that might be triggered by a place, a person, a relationship or some form of meditation. He then went on to add that *the embryo then begins to grow and evolve, governed only by irrational laws (or so it seems) – laws of the imagination, of the aesthetic sense and of emotion.* He went so far in this mystical denial of conscious intent on the writer's part as to say that it was to his critics that he owed most of his knowledge about the aims and ideas of his work. Asked what he wanted to say in the totality of his work, he answered: *It may be that I did not mean to say anything, but only drew comfort from making certain motions and emitting certain noises in a certain order which gave a semblance of purpose and signified, as it should of necessity, certain things. But if those things had been firm and clear, I would have preferred to present them in a different manner. Believe me – art is but the creation of life.*[73]

In 1989, Mahfouz was among 80 Arab intellectuals who signed a statement condemning the fatwa issued by the Iranian leader Ayatollah Khomeini against Salman Rushdie for *The Satanic Verses*. Death threats against him from Islamic fundamentalists followed, including one from the New York-based Shaykh Omar Abdul-Rahman, the blind leader of al-Gama'a al-Islamiyya, a militant Islamist movement in Egypt responsible for many acts of violence, accusing him of blasphemy in *Children of the Alley*. It was this condemnation that lead to the murder attempt on Mahfouz in 1994. The next year the Shaykh was jailed for life in the United States for 'Seditious Conspiracy' for his involvement in the first bomb attack on the World Trade Center in 1993.

A modest and very approachable man all his life, the international fame sprung on him overnight when he was declared a Nobel laureate in 1988 had little influence on his lifestyle and daily routine. Revered and honoured by both the Egyptian state and the man-in-the-street (who may or may not have read one of his novels) as an icon of the nation, he was not in his old age to be spared the wrath of religious fanaticism which characterised the violent decades of the 1980s and 1990s in Egypt. On 14 October 1994 he barely survived a murder attempt. The young man who stabbed him in the neck cited his authorship of the 'blasphemous' *Children of the Alley*, a novel written some 35 years earlier, as cause, while admitting not having read it. As a result of the injury, Mahfouz lost the use of his right arm and with it the ability to write, until physiotherapy and characteristic dogged persistence restored some use to it a year later.[74] Another consequence was Mahfouz's reluctant acceptance of what he had previously declined as a fetter on his freedom of movement:

24-hour police protection.[75] The last 15 years of the author's life saw a decline in the volume if not the quality of his creativity. His last novel, *Qushtumur Café*, was published in 1988, and his last collection of short stories, *Sada al-nisyan* (The Echo of Oblivion), in 1999. In *Echoes of an Autobiography* (1994) and in *Ahlam fatrat al-naqaha* (Dreams of Convalescence, 2006, or just *The Dreams*, as it is titled in the English translation which appeared in 2004 before the Arabic, and its sequel, *Dreams of Departure*, 2007), Mahfouz quietly invented in the last years of his long life a new genre, which I will call 'the aphoristic or parabolic narrative' for the lack of a better name, and of which more is to be said later. Mahfouz died in hospital on 30 August 2006, aged 94, after a three-week illness.[76]

Naguib Mahfouz and Ancient Egypt

Mahfouz's career as a novelist began with three novels set in Ancient Egypt: *Khufu's Wisdom*, *Rhadopis of Nubia* and *Thebes at War*, published in 1939, 1943 and 1944 respectively. However, his preoccupation with the history of Ancient Egypt went back several years further to 1931 when, still a student, he published a translation of an English text with the title *Ancient Egypt*[77] by one James Baikie. The original was published in London in 1912 as part of a series entitled 'Peeps at Many Lands'[78] aimed apparently at young readers in English. The translation, on the other hand, with the title *Misr al-qadima*[79] appeared in the 'Publications of *al-Majalla al-jadida*' (The New Review) published by Salama Musa,[80] who, as we have seen, encouraged Mahfouz at the beginning of his career.

The book describes in a simple, narrative style the various aspects of Ancient Egyptian life. Why did he translate the book (his one and only translation)? The answer he gave was that it was an exercise undertaken to improve his English.[81] But this does not explain why he chose a book with this subject-matter in particular. The choice must have been dictated by his growing interest in the history of Ancient Egypt which was only a few years later to be expressed more extensively. This interest must also be placed within the context of a main intellectual current at the time which found in the face of foreign rule a sense of national pride in Ancient Egyptian history. Elementary as the translated book is, there is no doubt that it had an influence on Mahfouz's early historical novels. Some of the details of daily life described in those books can easily be traced back to this source. In fact the entire plot of Mahfouz's first novel *Khufu's Wisdom* is taken from Chapter 7 in the book which gives an account of some Ancient Egyptian legends.

All three novels, though still highly readable as historical romances, bear the marks of an apprentice artist who, even when he finished the third of them, had not yet completely mastered the tools of his craft. *Khufu's Wisdom* (1939) is set during the reign of Khufu (Cheops), builder of the Great Pyramid and second king of the Fourth Dynasty in the time of the Old Kingdom. The action begins when one day Khufu asks a soothsayer how long his posterity was to reign over Egypt. The soothsayer answers that though the king himself was to rule undisturbed until the last day of his life, none of his descendants would sit on the throne after him, but rather a boy just born to a priest of the god Ra. The king sets out immediately at the head of a military campaign to protect his throne against the young would-be usurper. Thus he is set on a collision course with the fates (the Arabic title of the novel translates as 'The Game of the Fates'), and Mahfouz has his first opportunity in fiction to demonstrate to his readers a tenet that was to remain central to his work, namely that man's rationalised world is never secure from the haphazard and destructive inter- ference of some mysterious force or law of existence. This force or law would take many forms and names in Mahfouz's work. It could be called fate, accident, chance, coincidence, time or death, but would always have the same effect – to upset man's plans and shake the foundation of his rational calculations for his life. This does not necessarily imply belief in the supernatural on Mahfouz's part. What he seems generally interested in is merely to record that the failure of human endeavour is not always comprehensible in the simple terms of cause and effect.

Needless to say Khufu, in the novel under discussion, rather than thwarting the designs of fate by killing the newborn babe is, by a supreme act of irony, made the very tool for the accomplishment of the prophecy: he kills the wrong baby and unwittingly saves the right one from further danger. Eventually, the young man whom Khufu would have murdered many years before saves him from murder at the hands of his own son and heir-apparent in an attempted *coup d'état.* In recognition of his loyalty and distinguished services, the king, who finally learns on his deathbed the identity of his saviour, appoints him successor to the throne. Thus the prophecy is fulfilled by the very man who once thought in his vanity that he could avert the preordained.

'A Man Reserves a Seat'.

The bus started its journey from Zeytoun at the same moment that a private car set forth from the owner's house in Helwan. Each varied the speed at which it was travelling, speeding along and then slowing down, and perhaps coming to a stop for a minute or more depending on the state of the traffic. They both, however, reached Station Square at the same time, and even had a slight accident, in which one of the bus's headlights was broken and the front of the car was scratched. A man was passing and was crushed between the two vehicles and died. He was crossing the square in order to book a seat on the train going to Upper Egypt.[82]

Naguib Mahfouz

Rhadopis of Nubia, Mahfouz's second novel, is set during the short reign of Merenre towards the end of the Sixth Dynasty of the Old Kingdom. The young Pharaoh of the novel is engaged in a power conflict with the clergy over their enormous land possessions. Meanwhile, accident (or should we say fate?) brings the king in contact with Rhadopis, the courtesan at whose feet the cream of the city's men lie prostrate. It is love at first sight – love which takes possession of the king to the detriment of the affairs of the state and the feelings and pride of the queen, his sister and wife. More tragically, the affair gives the clergy a moral weapon to use against their opponent, who is finally killed in a popular uprising which he bravely faces without protection. True to romantic form, Rhadopis commits suicide with poison. The novel, like *Khufu's Wisdom*, is centrally built on coincidence. Life is again shown to be a frolic of fate, now assuming the form of an eagle which carries away Rhadopis' sandal and drops it in Pharaoh's lap, thus offering him the bait of love and eventually death.

Thebes at War, Mahfouz's third novel, deals with the struggle of the Egyptians against the foreign rule of the Hyksos, the invaders from Asia, who ruled Lower Egypt for around a hundred years in the 16th century BC. The action of the novel spans some 12 years and the reign of three Pharaohs until Egypt is finally and fully liberated under the leadership of King Ahmose, later known in history as the founder of the Eighteenth Dynasty. The heroic, nationalistic line of the plot is further complicated by a love story between the victorious King Ahmose and Princess Amenridis, the captive daughter of the vanquished Hyksos king Apophis, a love which he will have to renounce in favour of duty. Structurally it is a better novel than its predecessors in that the action does not depend on coincidence, and conflict between human wills takes precedence over conflict between man and fate. Altogether *Thebes at War* represents a movement forward for Mahfouz as a novelist. It is the most mature and balanced of his early historical trio. It is the nearest we get to a moral conflict when near the end King Ahmose is faced with the choice between keeping his beloved captive, the daughter of the Hyksos king, and releasing her in return for 30,000 Egyptian captives and a peaceful retreat into the desert by the Hyksos. The Hyksos princess reminds Ahmose that though kings enjoy the best in life, they also shoulder the heaviest duties. Nor was she prepared to forget her duty towards her vanquished father. Both Ahmose and Amenridis are shown here as Mahfouz's foils to Merenre and Rhadopis in the previous novel where love triumphed over duty. There, 'the heaviest duties' are forgotten, while 'the best in life' is enjoyed to the full. This is not permissible in Mahfouz's moral code, which is why Merenre and Rhadopis end tragically, whereas Ahmose and Amenridis go their separate ways, unhappy but ennobled and made wiser by the pain of their sacrifice. From this point on this moral code is always observed in the novelist's world: slaves of passion and self-interest will always fall, and those who uphold duty will always survive and prosper.

When Mahfouz published *Thebes at War* in 1944, he was to leave behind the history of Ancient Egypt for the next 40 years or so. According to him, before he started writing his historical novels, he had spent several years researching Ancient Egyptian history and had prepared the plans of up to 40 novels on the subject. After the first three, however, the whole project was to be abandoned and contemporary society was to claim his undivided attention. The impulse had been lost and he came to realise that history was no longer able to offer a medium for what he wanted to say in his fiction.[83] This proved to be the case for the next 39 years, which encompassed some 25 novels and 10 short-story collections. Then in 1983 Mahfouz surprised his readers by rediscovering the usefulness of history as a medium for expressing himself on the present: he published a book entitled *Before the Throne* with the subtitle 'A debate with Egypt's men from Menes to Anwar Sadat'. The book is a consideration of Egypt's political history. It stretches back in time some 5,000 years and starts at the beginning with Menes, the great king of the First Dynasty who united Upper and Lower Egypt into one kingdom, and thence works its way up to the assassination of Sadat in 1981. The 'Throne' of the title is that of Osiris, god of the underworld, before whom are brought all past rulers of Egypt for judgement according to their national deeds. It is a difficult book to classify, being unlike anything previously or since written by Mahfouz. It certainly is not a historical novel, nor is it a scholarly book of history in spite of its strict adherence to historical fact. Based mainly on dialogue rather than narration, it uses a fictitious dramatic situation (i.e. the underworld trial) to bring into focus a certain vision of Egyptian history in its entirety.

Whatever the form of the book, its content is invaluable as the writer's pronouncement on his age placed in historical perspective. Mahfouz's division of eternity follows Dante's paradigm in the *Divine Comedy*: Hell, Purgatory and Heaven. Viewing the book as a whole, it is not difficult to determine the author's yardstick (for he is the real judge here, rather than Osiris) in judging Egypt's rulers throughout history. Those who go to Heaven are the strong rulers who maintained the country's independence and national unity, their personal shortcomings forgiven in return. Those who go to Hell are selfish and weak rulers who favoured their personal interests over their country's and put at risk its unity and security through bad policy and neglect. As for those who go to Purgatory, they are rulers who were well-meaning but were faced with circumstances beyond their power or ability. The spectrum of the book is as vast as the period it purports to cover, but throughout, the past is continuously interpreted in terms of the present and vice versa with the result that there emerges in the end a sense of the unity of history and a unique failure to learn from it.

A good example is the trial of Nasser, for whom Mahfouz evidently has more rebuke than praise. According to the regulations of Osiris's court, rulers accorded a place in heaven automatically occupy a seat as members of the jury, as it were, and are involved in trying subsequent rulers. Thus we have Mustafa al-Nahhas (1879–1965), the great Wafdist leader thrown into oblivion by Nasser after a quarter of a century at the head of the Egyptian national struggle before 1952, railing at Nasser: 'You did away with freedom and human rights. I do not deny that you brought security for the poor, but you were the destruction of the intellectuals – the vanguard of the nation. They were detained, imprisoned and killed indiscriminately until they lost their sense of human dignity and initiative ... If you were only more moderate in your ambitions! Developing the Egyptian village was more important than adopting the revolutions of the world; sponsoring scientific research was more important than the Yemen campaign; fighting illiteracy was more important than fighting international imperialism. Alas! You have lost the country an opportunity which it had never had before.'[84] This outburst is evidently Mahfouz's final judgement on the Nasser era; it is the culmination of all the hints and lesser pronouncements he had been making in his fiction since the early 1960s, and as such it comes as no surprise. It is the pained lamentation of a liberal, socially-committed writer who witnessed the demise of freedom and hopes of progress at the very hands of the regime that initially promised to achieve them. Nasser is eventually admitted to Heaven, but significantly not before some hesitation on the part of Osiris who tells him: 'Few people have served their country as you have and fewer still have damaged it as you have'.[85] By comparison Sadat's trial is a 'white-wash'. He is quickly acquitted and recommended to be sent to Heaven on the claim that his reign was mainly devoted to the task of trying to put right the mess he inherited from Nasser.

Mahfouz was yet to tell another major Ancient Egyptian story before completely finishing with the genre. In an interview given in 1973 he listed some subjects which were abandoned when he decided to switch from history to the modern social scene. One of these subjects which he considered to be 'very important' was Akhenaten,[86] the Eighteenth Dynasty monarch who ruled Egypt some 14 centuries bc and preached a new religious cult based on the worship of the one god, Aten, symbolised by the sun disc. Little did Mahfouz know then that more than 20 years later this subject was actually to be written and used to elucidate the present.

The novel, whose title evokes the king-prophet, is *Akhenaten: Dweller in Truth* (1985). It takes the form of a quest for the truth about the king. The narrator is a young historian from the generation born after his fall. In his boyhood he was taught that the king had been an 'apostate' (*mariq*), whose policies had brought division and destruction to the country. Now he wants to discover

Mahfouz at work

the truth for himself and thus he embarks on a series of interviews with important men and women who were contemporaries of Akhenaten and who either supported or opposed him at the time. Through these interviews there emerges a picture of Akhenaten which oscillates between holiness and madness, strength of will and effeminacy, tolerance and fanaticism, according to the point of view. Mahfouz portrays Akhenaten in idealistic terms – he is at once a sensitive poet, a mystic who experienced a moment of divine revelation and a prophet who calls his people to a faith based on love and peace. On the other hand he is also pictured as a ruler guilty of the neglect of the affairs of state and spreading division among his people through his fanaticism and persecution of religious non-conformists. Faced with a situation which has deteriorated, Akhenaten asks the advice of his chief general, who recommends a declaration of the freedom of worship. This liberal call falls, however, on deaf ears and the king persists in imposing his religious dogma on the affairs of the state until the sad end.

Written in the 1980s at a time of worldwide Islamic resurgence when the influence of the Islamic Republic in Iran was at its highest, and when religious fundamentalism in Egypt was calling for *jihad* (holy war) against the 'infidel' State and the adoption of *sharia* (religious law) in a society which, on the one hand, is largely secularised, and which, on the other, has a sizeable Christian minority, the ancient message of the tragedy of Akhenaten could not have sounded more contemporary. Nor was Mafouz unwilling to say explicitly in an interview what he thought of him in the course of commenting on the novel. He argued that Akhenaten may have been an idealist with a particular calling, but that his approach to reality was erroneous: *It is not the business of a preacher to utilise material power to spread his belief.*[87] This late historical novel by Mahfouz, written more than 40 years since the three with which he started his career is, by comparison, a highly accomplished work; a work by an artist at the height of his career.

Naguib Mahfouz and Modern Egypt: The Realistic Novels before *The Cairo Trilogy*

In 1945 Mahfouz published *Khan al-Khalili*,[88] thereby marking a shift of interest from ancient history to contemporary social reality. *Khan al-Khalili* was to be the first of a series of novels dealing, in the best traditions of realism and naturalism, with contemporary Egyptian society before the 1952 revolution. It was followed in rapid succession by *Cairo Modern* in 1946, *Midaq Alley* in 1947, *The Mirage* in 1948, and *The Beginning and the End* in 1949. Throughout this phase of his writing, which culminated in the publication of *The Trilogy* in 1956–7, Mahfouz appeared to have one particular theme which ran through all of them, sometimes obviously, sometimes not so obviously: the conflict between old and new, or past and present; in other words, the conflict between two value systems, one wallowing in the security of age-old tradition, and the other attracted to Western modernity with all its attendant perils. In all these novels Mahfouz appears highly sensitive to the tragic potential of such conflict to both individual and society.

Khan al-Khalili spans one year in the life of a Cairene family during the Second World War: from September 1941 to August 1942 during the height of German air-raids on Cairo. The family decide to escape from the modern quarter of al-Sakakini where they have lived for a long time to the old religious quarter of Khan al-Khalili in the neighbourhood of the shrine of al-Husayn, grandson of the Prophet Muhammad. They believe that al-Husayn will protect the area and that the Germans should know better than to bomb Muslim holy places. The symbolic aspect of the family's flight can hardly be missed: it is a flight from the dangers of the new to the presumed safety of the old.

Mahfouz uses two of his characters to advocate respectively the old and the new (a technique that he used again in *Cairo Modern* as well as *The Trilogy* III). The old is represented by Ahmad Akif, the eldest son and provider for the family, while the new is represented by Ahmad Rashid, a lawyer who frequents the same local café as Akif, where they engage in endless conversations. The lawyer is a well-read socialist who believes that modern society has no place for religion and that social progress can only be achieved through dependence on science. The advocate of the old is a frustrated and introverted government clerk with little formal education. He has, however, read extensively in traditional religious literature, but when it comes to modern thought, he is so ignorant he has not even heard of Marx, Freud or Nietzsche. The juxtaposition of the old and the new, represented respectively by Ahmad Akif and Ahmad Rashid is borne out by their contrasted attitudes towards the old quarter of al-Husayn, which is described as having 'resisted modern civilisation, countering its madness with wisdom, complexity with simplicity and realism with dreaminess'.[89] These qualities seem to match those of Ahmad Akif, the advocate of the old, who lives in a world of his own making, steeped in the wisdom of the past and totally ignorant of the complex thought of the present, while Ahmad Rashid, the advocate of change, sees in the old quarter nothing but 'derelict remnants … only filth … that ought to be razed to the ground to give people the chance to live healthily and happily'.[90] Mahfouz's answer to the dilemma posed by this duality is uncertain. Both characters are portrayed negatively, which makes it difficult to assume an authorial preference for either model. It may well be that the tension in characterisation reflects the tension in the novelist's soul before the stark choices available to the modern Egyptian.

On the other hand, Mahfouz's fascination with the wayward frolics of fate continues in this novel. For the family which runs away from death in Sakakini finds it lurking patiently for its arrival in Khan al-Khalili to snatch away Rushdi, the younger son, who dies of tuberculosis contracted during their year there: surviving the air-raids of a world war does not mean that fate cannot get you by some other means.

The portrayal of Ahmad Akif is particularly problematic. The author seems to have an ambivalent attitude towards him, at once showing him as a hollow laughable character, and a man with a sublime sense of duty who sacrifices his career and personal happiness for the sake of his parents and younger brother. As such he is in fact the model of a character type that will always command the respect of the author and will usually be saved from the harshness of his poetic justice. Indeed, he survives here and is left at the end with the author's reward of a promised job promotion and the prospect of a suitable marriage after long celibacy into middle age. If this is the case, why the insistence throughout on the negative side of his character? The answer to this question must lie solely with the imperfections of the young artist's craft.

In *Khan al-Khalili* the cases for the old and the new appeared largely to be presented in a social vacuum since the novel lacked a socio-political theme, while the arguments for each case were confined to the idle talk of two unevenly portrayed characters sitting at a café. *Cairo Modern*, published a year later in 1946, was an improvement. A socio-political theme was introduced so that the choice between different systems is made a matter of relevance and vital importance.

Cairo Modern is indeed about moral choices, on both the individual and the social levels. In fact, in Mahfouz's world individual

Mahfouz leaving one of his favourite cafés, the Ali Baba on Tahrir Square

morality and social morality are indivisible; they are the two sides of one coin. Thus an individual who is solely concerned with his own personal salvation, showing no regard for other individuals in his immediate environment or in society at large, is an accursed self-seeker who can hope for no place in Mahfouz's heaven. Mahgub Abd al-Da'im, the main protagonist of the novel, is the unrivalled archetype of this kind of character which was to figure again and again in Mahfouz's social panorama. His philosophy, as defined by the omniscient author, is 'to liberate oneself from everything, from values, ideals, beliefs and principles: from the social heritage altogether'.[91] True to naturalistic form, the author tells us that Mahgub owed his philosophy to his own disposition, emphasised by his poor background, which meant that he virtually grew up 'in the street'.[92] These, then, are the effects of temperament and the environment, though temperament is not shown here to be the product of heredity. It is against a backdrop of extreme poverty and widespread unemployment and political and official corruption in 1930s Cairo that we are made to witness Mahgub's moral disintegration, which turns him into a private pimp who trades his wife in return for a government post that would otherwise have been difficult to attain. Here we are faced with a problem. On the one hand, Mahfouz seems concerned with the question of social evil and its corrupting influence on the individual. On the other hand, however, he insists in his portrayal of Mahgub on his utter depravity and complete moral nihilism from the outset – a fact which detracts from the force of the author's blaming of society for the downfall of the individual. In later novels Mahfouz was to solve this problem through more balanced portrayals of his protagonists and tighter linkage between social injustice and the individual's fall.

The novel, however, presents us with two more protagonists who are equally pure, altruistic and desirous of being instrumental in the reform of their society: one a Muslim fundamentalist and the other a socialist. While they are both foils to the amoral character of Mahgub, they are themselves at odds, with no hope of reconciliation. They both agree on the importance of moral principles for man, but they radically differ on the nature and source of these principles. The fundamentalist is content with the principles of Islam 'laid down by God Almighty', as he puts it, whereas the socialist's principles consist in 'belief in science instead of superstition, society instead of heaven, and socialism instead of competition'[93] – words which echo those of Ahmad Rashid in the previous novel. (In fact, this duo, a major improvement on the pair in *Khan al-Khalili*, will be re-introduced for the third time in *The Trilogy* III under the names of the two brothers Ahmad and Abd al-Mun'im Shawkat.) Which, then, of the two opposed social visions does the author favour? Unlike in *Khan al-Khalili*, Mahfouz's portrayal of the two characters here leaves no doubt as to where the author's

Mahfouz on the streets of old Cairo

sympathy lies. The fundamentalist is portrayed negatively as a sharp-tempered fanatic, given to loneliness, capable of demented cruelty and lacking a sense of humour.[94] Against this gruesome portrait is juxtaposed the more human one of the socialist who is shown as possessed of a sociable and genial nature, with his time fairly divided among activities such as reading, sports, intellectual debate, travel and meeting his girlfriend.

Mahfouz's next novel, *Midaq Alley* (1947), takes us back to the streets and folk of old Cairo that he introduced us to earlier in *Khan al-Khalili.* The country is still in the grip of the Second World War, though at a more developed stage than that shown in *Khan al-Khalili.* Textual evidence suggests late 1944 or early 1945. The war actually ends during the course of the action of the novel. *Midaq Alley* is in a sense the inversion of the metaphor created by *Khan al-Khalili.* The latter showed us the vanity of seeking refuge in the past from the threat of the new. *Midaq Alley*, in contrast, reveals to us the horrors attendant on the flight from the past to the present. The outcome of both is shown to be calamitous. Torn between past and present, the modern Egyptian seems to stand paralysed without a future, and the pessimism expressed in *Khan al-Khalili* is even bleaker in *Midaq Alley.*

Midaq Alley is a novel with many protagonists, all enjoying the almost equal attention of their creator with the exception of the heroine, Hamida, who is perhaps somewhat more central to the book than the rest. The book is episodic in structure, lacking a central plot and held together mainly through the unities of place and theme. The place is of course the old alley of the title and the theme is that of change, of the painful conflict between old and new whose theatre is the soul of man. This theme is introduced soon after the opening lines of the novel and sets the pace of the entire work from that moment on. We see the old poet, who has entertained his audience at the café in the alley for many years by singing for them the exploits of traditional Arab folk heroes, being mercilessly ousted by an act of rejection of the past, an act of modernisation: a radio set is being fitted in the café which cannot accommodate both. An important factor is thus symbolically established from the outset: the old and the new cannot coexist. By dint of this yardstick the fates of characters in the novel faced with the necessity of choosing will be decided: those who sell their souls to modernity without a moment's hesitation and pay the price with unflinching eyes, like Hamida, will be spared, but those who waver and stop to look behind, like Abbas al-Hulw, will perish. As in *Khan al-Khalili*, modernity here is represented by the war. There, people fled from the destruction of modernity to the illusory safety of the past, while here they escape from the poverty, filth and death-in-life of the old alley to the promise of a new life offered by employment in the camps of the British army.

Hamida, however, enters the service of the army in a somewhat different and unofficial capacity: she joins the sex industry catering to the needs of Allied soldiers. Long before she makes her final choice, her contempt for the alley with all it stands for is total and complete. Her initial acceptance of Abbas', the alley's barber, offer of love and marriage was made out of circumstantial necessity, the barber being the best the alley could offer. Even so, it was only made after the young man had decided to make the sacrificial journey to the British camps to bring back money and the promise of life out of the alley. Thus when the wealthy old merchant, Salim Alwan, who does not belong to the alley (either by class or means) but only has his storehouse in it, asks for her hand in marriage to satisfy a nagging lust, she drops the barber without so much as a moment's thought. The immediacy and ease with which she does this illustrates her total disdain for the value system of the alley, which stands in the way of her aspiration for material success. The project, however, comes to nothing as fate strikes the merchant with a heart attack that leaves him nearly dead. But there is no going back to Abbas: Hamida now understands herself better and knows that her fulfilment lies in a different world, well outside the scope of the alley. Thus when Ibrahim Faraj, suave pimp and emissary of that world to her, makes his appearance and utters his seductive words: 'This place is not where you belong and these people are not your people. You are different – you are a stranger here',[95] he is only voicing her own conviction. Hamida, with all her shocking qualities, appears indeed to be Mahfouz's answer, *malgré lui*, to the dilemma of past and present, old and new, East and West, religion and secularism or any other name that it might be called by. In the novel she is the only character who succeeds in tearing herself away irrevocably from the alley. She thrives on it without regrets – even after an attempt is made on her life by the past (in the person of her ex-fiancé, Abbas), the author allows her to live unscathed and to continue to thrive, while her poor attacker is crushed to death under the feet of drunken and enraged British soldiers. She succeeds because she is ready to pay the price in full – her old soul, her old *honour*, the quintessential symbol of the old morality and the entire cultural fabric behind it. Hamida, with her ambition, adventurism, individualism, entrepreneurialism, solipsism, shamelessness, bellicosity, freedom from emotionalism, practical (if not philosophical) atheism etc, symbolises in fact many of the intellectual values which made the modern West. The very fact that Hamida can only free herself from the past at the expense of becoming a prostitute in the service of Western soldiers is not without significance on the symbolic level: for is not the renunciation by a culture of its traditional and historic identity in return for the 'light, wealth and power' of modernity an act of prostitution *in extremis*?

In *The Mirage* (1948)[96] Mahfouz takes a momentary break from old Cairo with its seedy streets to pay a visit to al-Manyal, a decent middle-class area in the south-west of the capital. With the change of habitat there comes naturally a change in the inhabitants: none of the poor company of Midaq Alley here, but a wealthy family of

Turkish descent. Unlike in *Khan al-Khalili* and *Midaq Alley*, the war has no part here to play and we are back at some undefined point in the 1930s. But above all our attention is diverted (or so it seems) from society to psyche – Mahfouz here appears to be concerned with the representation of psychological rather than physical or naturalistic reality. In the process of doing so he vacates his hitherto habitual position of omniscient narrator and hands us over to his protagonist, Kamil Ru'ba Laz, to tell his own story and to reveal to us other characters from his solitary point of view.

The novel is a cathartic journey into the past by the protagonist-narrator. It is a long and probing look inward to understand the make-up of his perturbed soul and the composition of the mesh of events and relationships that led to catastrophe. The catastrophe consists in the tragic death within hours of each other of both his wife and his mother: Kamil believes that he was instrumental in both deaths. About 28 years of age, he traces the tragedy back to its beginnings in his infancy. He was the youngest child of a divorced mother already deprived of seeing her two other children by their father, who has legal custody of them. She thus concentrates all her affection on him. The child is raised in an abnormal atmosphere completely isolated from the outside world by his over-loving, over-protective mother. The boy grows up a social misfit without self-confidence, without friends, and a failure at school. He has no relationships with girls and his only sexual outlet until he is married at the age of 26 is masturbation. Marriage, however, suggests that he is sexually impotent, but later an affair with an ugly middle-aged woman proves the opposite (an ugly maid-servant had initiated him into sex as a young boy, but they were found out by the mother and he was left with a guilt complex). It turns out that he associated his beautiful wife with his mother and was thus unable to 'defile' her sexually – only an ugly and earthy woman (like the servant of his childhood) could trigger sexual response in him. His frustrated wife finally has an affair and dies during an abortion performed on her by her cousin, a doctor, the very man with whom she had the affair. Kamil knows the truth only after her death. In his despair he blames everything on his mother, whose weak heart collapses under the pressure of the shocking news and the sudden barrage of hatred from her son.

Critics have tended to see the book for the one thing that it certainly is: a psychological novel offering a study of an acute case of the Oedipus complex and following the techniques of psychoanalysis used by Freud. Those who read it as such and no more see it as an unclassifiable oddity in the work of Mahfouz. However, I would argue that, read at a deeper level, *The Mirage* will fall well within the mainstream of Mahfouz's social and intellectual concerns. It should not be difficult to see in Kamil's psychological illness a metaphor for a whole society fixated on its cultural past and too *impotent* to free itself from it. As such *The Mirage* falls in line thematically with *Khan al-Khalili* and *Midaq Alley*. The mother is established from the beginning as a symbol of a haunting past, a figure that is dead but will not lie down. 'She is dead to this world,' writes Kamil of her, 'but she still resides in my depths ... always behind my hopes and pains, my loves and hates.'[97] What we have here is the same tension between past and present, old and new that we have experienced in the earlier novels re-dressed in the guise of a psychological narrative. It would seem that at that time Mahfouz's preoccupation with the subject infiltrated, consciously or subconsciously, any story he wanted to tell.

The Beginning and the End (1949) is set in the Cairo of the mid-1930s, and more particularly in the poor parts of the old suburb of Shubra. The novel brings a depth of vision and a mastery of technique to concerns already familiar from his four previous novels. Fate, whose supreme role in the world of Mahfouz was established in his first novel, *Khufu's Wisdom*, and whose deadly blows have afflicted Rushdi Akif in *Khan al-Khalili* and Abbas al-Hulw in *Midaq Alley*, is here crowned as unrivalled lord over the life and aspirations of mankind, a force which, in the words of one character, 'grinds and devours' its victims.[98] The whimsical acts of fate start just before the beginning of the action by snatching away the life of the head of the lower-middle-class family whose fortunes (or rather misfortunes) constitute the subject-matter of the book. Already of limited means, the family of a widow, three sons and a daughter, is now reduced to measures of extreme austerity in order barely to survive on the meagre pension left by the deceased father. The death of the father, however, was only fate's opening skirmish and the narrative maintains an atmosphere of bleakness and a sense of impending doom that leaves the reader in no doubt that more disasters are to come. Fate, however, is in no hurry; it likes to do a good job. Thus the action of the novel spans some four years, during which the proud daughter of a pro-fessional family is reduced first to seamstress and then whore; the eldest son to a night-club bouncer and drug-trafficker; and the second son to giving up his hopes of higher education to become a petty clerk. The youngest, however, seems, thanks to the help and sacrifices of the rest of the family, set to escape misfortune – or does he? He graduates as an army officer and just as he prepares to begin a new life, fate smiles its knowing smile and deals the final blow for which the scene has long been set. With alarming speed the young aspirant's world falls to pieces: a marriage proposal from him is rejected by an upper-class family on account of his humble origins; his eldest brother is being pursued by the police as a wanted criminal; and his sister is arrested in a brothel. Unable to face the scandal, he forces her to commit suicide before he follows suit.

In the novel fate as a supernatural power has only a limited role to play, namely through the death of the father at the beginning. But the rest of the tragedy does not simply follow from this super-natural interference in the life of humans. After this initial act, fate actually chooses to work through perfectly reasonable means, namely individual temperament and, to a much lesser extent, society. Hussein, the middle brother, explains to his younger brother, Hassanein, that while God 'may be responsible for the death of our father, he can by no means be responsible for the inadequacy of the pension he left us'.[99] What is at issue here is the question of social justice; death may be a supernatural evil, but social injustice is entirely man-made and therefore curable. It is a form of fate that can be fought and vanquished. Many critics have been misguided by the poverty of the family as well as the words just quoted above into blaming the subsequent tragedies on society or, as it were, social fate. Mahfouz himself has indeed misleadingly argued that the real villain of the novel is Ismail Sidqi (1875–1950), the unpopular prime minister of Egypt at the time.[100] In fact Sidqi is not even mentioned in the novel, nor does the plot have a political background in any significant measure. All there is are marginal references to demonstrations against the British and the signing of the treaty of independence in 1936. The novel in fact is an indictment of human nature, of the way we are made: character is fate. The insistence throughout on Nefisa's physical ugliness and passionate sexuality leave little room for the possibility of blaming her fall on society. Even in a social utopia, she would still be ugly, without a husband, and with a sexual urge demanding satisfaction. The same goes for Hassanein, to whom society gives ample leeway by allowing him to rise against considerable odds to an officer's position. It is his own egoism, excessive ambition, impatient nature and denial of his own class that bring about his downfall. By contrast, Hussein is optimistic, patient and self-denying, and is thus a foil to the character of his brother. These qualities save him from destruction, even though society has been less kind to him than to his brother, forcing him to sacrifice his higher education in order to support his family. Fate in *The Beginning and the End* is thus first and foremost temperament. As Hassanein puts it in his final moment of revelation before jumping into the Nile, 'There is something fundamentally wrong with our nature – I don't know what it is but it has destroyed me'.[101] Mahfouz is undoubtedly also concerned with the shortcomings of society which make such conditions as his characters live in possible, but his insistence on their own hereditary weaknesses, both physical and temperamental, largely neutralises his condemnation of society: what we have here is a lopsided version of naturalism. Three novels later, his vision of society and the individual is still as uncomfortable as it was in *Cairo Modern*.

Hassanein is by far Mahfouz's most sophisticated rendering of the ultimate egoist. Unlike his prototype, Mahgub of *Cairo Modern*, he is a tragic hero who commands our full sympathy in his heroic and fatal struggle against the past. Painfully class-conscious and aspiring to mobility across the social strata, once he becomes an army officer he wants to reshape his life as if the past had never existed. He wants 'a new past, a new house, a new grave [for his dead father], a new family, plenty of money and a glamorous life'.[102] The past, however, haunts him in the shape of his own gnawing fears and worries, his incurable insecurity and most palpably through his fallen brother and sister. The past clings to him like a leech, while the new life symbolised by the upper class rejects him with contempt. In his final moment of truth, his thoughts run like this: 'I have always wanted to erase the past, but the past has swallowed the present – the past has been none else but me.'[103] Mahfouz is obviously still agonising over the theme of past and present. Hassanein's conflict with the past here is yet another episode in the series of novels which began in *Cairo Modern* with Mahgub Abd al-Da'im's wholesale jettisoning of the values of the past. Through metaphor after metaphor, the novelist's belief in the non-viability of a total rejection of the past is reaffirmed. His best compromise appears to be the character of Hussein in the present novel. He is a composite of the Islamist and the socialist models of *Cairo Modern*, believing in 'a socialist system which does not conflict with religion, family or morality'.[104] Unlike his brother, Hussein is also a pragmatist who realises that 'if we could economise in our dreams or take our inspiration from reality in creating those dreams, we would not be sorry or disappointed'.[105] He is a man of integrity, duty, persistence, moderation and gradual progress – he is no rebel, and with him the *status quo* could go on indefinitely. But the book is not about him. It is about Hassanein, the fire that feeds upon itself. He lacks Hassanein's vivacity and lustre and he fails to strike a spark in our imagination. It is only half-heartedly that Mahfouz offers him as an alternative.

The Cairo Trilogy and other Egyptian Sagas

A preoccupation with time is at the centre of Mahfouz's work. A thought that is uppermost in his writings is how time affects the individual and the community and how human memory relates to external time. Mahfouz wrote three novels in which time is a prime concern, all of which are also *romans fleuves* in the sense that they are concerned with the examination of the changing conditions of life for individuals and society across a succession of generations in a given family. Those are *The Cairo Trilogy* (1956–7), and the much later *There Only Remains an Hour* (1982) and *The Day the Leader was Killed* (1985). However, of the three it is only *The Cairo Trilogy* which is written on the grand scale associated with this type of novel, as established by such European masters as Balzac, Zola and Mann. The other two are *romans fleuves* of a lesser order, cramming too many events and characters into what are very short novels, and more inclined towards the quick reportage of change than in its detailed representation and the creation of a real sense of the passage of time.

Mahfouz was explicit about his philosophy of time, which, as we have seen in the first chapter of this book, was influenced by the ideas of Henri Bergson. In the course of discussing techniques of dealing with time in the novel, Mahfouz contrasted 'logical time' with 'psychological time' and came out mostly in favour of the first. He insisted on the historicity of time and argued that *time represents the evolutionary spirit of man; it perpetuates the human experience* of life. Therefore, while it may mean extinction to the individual, it means eternity for the species. In another statement he reaffirmed the same point: *My contemplation of time and death has taught me to regard them with the eye of collective man and not* [that of] *the individual. To the individual they are calamitous, but to collective man a mere illusion ... What can death do to human society? Nothing. At any moment you will find society bustling with millions* [of lives]. But if Mahfouz viewed the relation between man and time as inevitably a tragic one on the individual level, he made it amply clear that he believed it need not be so on the social level. Indeed, so optimistic was he about human progress that he did not preclude the possibility of a final human victory over time and death, as the following statement suggests: *As long as life ends in disability and death, it is a tragedy ... Even those who see it as a crossroad to the hereafter will have to accept that the first part of it is a tragedy ... But the tragedy of life is a complex one ... For when we think of life as merely existence, we tend to see it only in the abstract terms of existence and non-existence. But when we think of it in terms of existence in society, we discover in it many artificial tragedies of man's own making, such as ignorance, poverty, exploitation, violence ... This justifies our emphasis on the tragedies of society, because these are ones that can be remedied, and because in the act of remedying them we create civilisation and progress. Indeed, progress might ameliorate the original tragedy* [i.e. death] *and might even conquer it altogether.*[106] These views will be useful to bear in mind in the course of examining *The Cairo Trilogy*, arguably Mahfouz's greatest work.

〜

According to Mahfouz *The Trilogy* took some seven years to prepare and write, starting from 1945 to April 1952 when it was completed. Originally it was written as one piece with the title *Palace Walk*, but Mahfouz's publisher rejected it on account of its excessive length. However, when what later came to be known as the first part of *The Trilogy* was successfully serialised in the then literary magazine *al-Risala al-jadida* (between April 1954 and April 1956), the publisher changed his mind and suggested to Mahfouz that he should divide the book into three parts with different titles. That was how the work became the trilogy, consisting of *Palace Walk*, *Palace of Desire* and *Sugar Street*.[107] While pursuing many of the themes of the earlier novels, particularly that of the conflict between old and new, *The Trilogy* takes the action back to an earlier point in time: 1917 and the years leading up to the popular revolution of 1919 and continuing through three generations of the protagonist-family to stop in 1944. The symbolic power of the dates is self-evident. The novel begins in the middle of a world war and terminates towards the end of another. The world is in the process of convulsive change and so is Egyptian society. Change is painful but inevitable. And change occurs in time which may be favourable to society, its benignity being embedded in the infinite hope attendant on its own infiniteness. Not so, alas, is time to the individual because here it is hopelessly finite and, as it inexorably advances, it can only hold the promise of death and decay. This novel is about time and man and the myriad nameless things that such a story would entail.

The 1,500 or so pages which constitute the three parts of *The Trilogy* are a powerful embodiment of Mahfouz's concept of time expounded above. At the end of the 28-year period spanned by the novel, the members of the Abd al-Jawwad family are in a poor state indeed, their fortunes ranging from shattered hopes (Kamal) and death-in-life (Aisha) to actual death (Fahmy). Conversely, the society to which these victims of time belong is seen at the end to be in much better shape than it was at the beginning: Egypt has survived two world wars partly fought on its soil and a revolution brutally put down by a great colonial power, has gained partial independence, and the national struggle which in Fahmy's generation had been limited to the issues of independence and constitutional government has been widened in Ahmad Shawkat's generation to include the issue of social justice as well. Thus while Fahmy, who was killed in the revolution, has been decaying in his grave for 26 years, Egypt has been steadily progressing on the course for which he and many other individuals died.

Mahfouz allocates the first 47 chapters of *Palace Walk*, roughly two-thirds of the book, to a description of the homely and the quotidian. We get to know all the members of the Abd al-Jawwad family in their daily routine. We see all the morning rituals: waking up, baking the bread, breakfast, the men going out to work or school and the women doing housework. We are also taken to the afternoon coffee gathering. We see Fahmy on the roof professing his love to their next-door neighbour, Maryam; the father in his shop and in his rowdy gatherings at night with his friends and their singing mistresses; Yasin in his obsessive pursuit of Zanuba; the little adventures of the young Kamal on his way back from school; the weddings of Aisha, Yasin and Khadija in succession. All this we see and much more. And it is this descriptive quality that gives the book, among other things, its documentary value. There is no other source, literary or otherwise, that records with such detail and liveliness the habits, sentiments and living environment of Cairene Egyptians at the beginning of the century.[108] Without the novelist's loving and observant eye much about that period that no longer exists would have gone unrecorded forever. Interesting in itself as this detailed record of the homely and the quotidian is, it has another function, namely to prepare the scene for the shattering impact of the approaching revolution. They and we will soon be shocked out of a false sense of security and continuity, and learn that no human condition can go on immune from the transgression of time and that when history convulses, the lives of individuals crack and crumble.

When the British authorities exile Saad Zaghloul, having refused him permission to travel to Paris to air the nation's demand for independence before the peace conference at Versailles in 1919, the revolution erupts and martial law is enforced. From that moment the life of the family is never the same again. The novel reveals to us gradually the build-up of public events, and as the pace of action is stepped up, the inevitable convergence of public and private reaches its tragic conclusion. The afternoon coffee gathering formerly reserved for innocent chat and the usual bickerings among brothers and sisters is now dominated by talk of politics and accounts of demonstrations and violent confrontations with soldiers. Everyone has something to tell whether it is the 10-year-old schoolboy Kamal, or the 19-year-old university student Fahmy, who is actively involved in distributing handbills and organising demonstrations and strikes. As the revolution escalates, the British decide to occupy the old quarter of al-Husayn (a focal point for revolutionary agitation) where the family lives. They camp right outside the family house. The household is thrown into confusion and for some time the family impose house-arrest on themselves because they do not know the intentions of the occupying force. Abd al-Jawwad's family is thus made to embody the condition of the entire nation and historical danger is seen to be as close to the individual as the front door of his own home. The consequences of such menacing proximity materialise without delay when we see the fearsome and much-respected patriarch, Abd al-Jawwad, arrested at gunpoint on his way home one night and forced most ignominiously to take part in refilling a trench dug earlier by rebels. Another consequence is the courtship of Maryam by a soldier. Her favourable response is witnessed and innocently publicised by the young Kamal, a fact which breaks the heart of Fahmy, who loves the girl and would have been engaged to her but for his father's objection. Yet another consequence is the near-lynching of Yasin at the al-Husayn Mosque when he is wrongly suspected by worshippers of being a spy for the British. These and many other small incidents bring home to the reader the true meaning of history (one not to be found in the annals of historians) as little units of time filled up by little units of people, the amalgamation of whose sufferings and deaths is what we later come to call a revolution or a war.

We all live through time, cataclysmic or ordinary, labouring under the illusion that its afflictions are things which befall others and not ourselves. Thus when the father learns of Fahmy's involvement in the revolution, he is shaken to the core: 'Had the flood reached his doorstep?' The revolution has had his support, financial and emotional, but when it comes to the involvement of one of his own sons, that is a different matter: 'It was as if they were a race unto themselves, standing outside the domain of history. He alone was the one to draw the limits for them, not the revolution, not the times and not other people.'[109] But alas! Such pride, such heroic defiance can only be in vain. Fahmy is killed in a demonstration: 'The times, the revolution and other people' pushed him far beyond the limits set for him by his father. He has become an *individual* brick in the edifice of *history*.

Fahmy may die as an individual and his death may bring infinite grief to his father and mother, causing the first to relinquish for five long years his night life of pleasure and the latter to age beyond her years, but this is not his end. Not quite, according to Mahfouz's philosophy of time. When a person has exhausted his units of individual time, he must depart from the scene and allow his inexhaustible stock of social or collective time to be used on his behalf *in absentia.* Thus Fahmy dies, but the national struggle does not cease and society benefits from his death and that of other individuals. The novelist underlines this meaning by resurrecting Fahmy in the image of another revolutionary in the next generation of the family, namely Ahmad Shawkat, his nephew, born years after his death. Some 25 years after the death of Fahmy, his reincarnation is sent to prison on account of his socialist views and active involvement in spreading them. Collective time has obviously carried the national struggle a step forward: the issue now is no longer just political freedom, but also social justice, and Ahmad Shawkat, like his old incarnation, is prepared to pay out of his *individual* time for the *public* cause. This is a moralistic view of the relationship between man and time and is at the very heart of Mahfouz's vision. There is no doubt that on the existential level he sees time as man's worst enemy and as such the battle against it becomes his first moral duty. The battle, however, is bound to be lost on the individual level since death is ineluctable. Our only hope in victory then is social or collective. Ahmad Shawkat sums it up neatly: 'The common duty of humanity is perpetual revolution which consists in the persistent endeavour to realise the will of life as represented in its evolution towards the highest ideal.'[110]

Time, however, does not need to call up revolutions, wars or any other form of historical cataclysm in order to inflict death and destruction on the lives of individuals. Cataclysmic time is only a heightened form of quotidian time, which is equally destructive. Cataclysmic time sees to those individuals who die in violent demonstrations, warlike actions, earthquakes, floods, etc, whereas quotidian time looks after those who die of old age, prolonged illness, accidents or for no comprehensible reason at all. Death, however, is only time's final and ironically merciful blow. What is really tragic is the time process in its daily unfolding as it leads up to death, i.e. the consciousness of the changing self and circumstances in time – ultimately, the consciousness that life is but death in progress. Ahmad Abd al-Jawwad is a good example. He is portrayed in almost superhuman terms. Physically a giant resplendent with health and beauty; an authoritarian patriarch at home, as much feared as loved; a successful merchant; an adored friend and lover; at once a libertine and a devout worshipper – a bundle of contradictions fused together in a harmonious and admirable whole that by just existing seemed temporarily to mock the very idea of Time. *Temporarily*, I said, because so things appear until time claims its due. After a long process of gradual deterioration begun after the death of his son Fahmy and extending over a period of some 20 years (amply illustrated in the book), this paragon of strength and vitality is reduced to a disabled bundle carried home like a child from an air-raid shelter by his son Kamal. The cycle is completed and the man has become a child again: that night after this final humiliation, he dies.

Unlike cataclysmic time, which has no pattern and can kill someone like Fahmy at the age of 19 without overtaxing human comprehension, quotidian time seems to work according to some sort of pattern, or so embattled humans imagine. People usually expect, despite their awareness of the inevitable end, a reasonable allowance of time in which to grow up, mature and fulfil themselves in life up to a point, within their means and circumstances before the laws of mutation and decay claim them. But time does not always oblige. A pattern it may have, but patterns have exceptions, and time patterns are no exception. Thus Aisha loses her youthful husband and her two young sons at one stroke. Typhoid does it. A few years later she loses her remaining daughter, who dies in childbirth within one year of her marriage. Aisha's sanity, which barely withstood the first breach of the pattern, collapses at the second. Grief gnaws at her heart and still in her thirties she becomes the living remnant of what not too long ago was an image of beauty and the love of life.

In real life death can seem quite accidental and totally without meaning except for the mundane affirmation of the fragility and transience of human existence. In Mahfouz, however, even when it looks most irrational, at closer view it will transpire that the author has imbued it with a subtle moral point. The tragedy of Aisha and her family is an example. In the expository sections of the novel there is an insistence (which is sustained at intervals throughout the novel) on her beauty on the one hand, and her uselessness on the other: 'She appeared in the midst of the family like a beautiful but useless symbol.'[111] She is also shown to be narcissistically obsessed with her beauty, always admiring her reflection in the mirror. She has a carefree temperament, singing or humming all the time in her beautiful voice and showing little interest in housework – all of which may appear to the ordinary eye as sins of a venial nature. But not according to the stern ethics of Mahfouz. What makes matters worse is that she gets married to one of the Shawkat brothers. The two brothers are portrayed by the novelist as the epitome of idleness. Of Turkish descent, they are without education and without jobs (in fact they profess their contempt for work), but with enough income from property to provide for a decent standard of living. Their days and nights are spent at home in sleep or useless activities (such as playing music in the case of Khalil, Aisha's husband). Naturally, they display no interest whatsoever in the turmoil of public life. As they advance in age, they continue to possess good health and young looks: they are described as 'the two amazing men who do not seem to change with time as though they stood outside its stream'.[112] Considering her natural tendencies, it is no wonder that Aisha, after marriage, 'was submerged in Shawkatism up to her neck'.[113] Na'ima, Aisha's daughter, is depicted as a replica of her mother. Her beauty is that of a 'pin-up girl',[114] and her eyes 'reflect a gentle and dreamy look washed in purity, a naivety and a sense of foreignness to this world'.[115] Like her mother, she is given, from her infancy, to singing and dancing and 'uselessness'. Now, 'standing outside the stream of time' watching life go by and enjoying oneself no matter what is an indulgence that real time might occasionally overlook, but, harnessed in the service of Mahfouzian morality, it would seldom be pardoned. Therefore the entire Khalil branch of the Shawkat family is wiped from the face of the earth, while Aisha, as a further punishment, is spared to muse upon her loss and die a slow death.

One might wonder why not as well kill off Ibrahim Shawkat,

Mahfouz in the old quarter of Cairo

Khalil's elder brother who got married to Khadija, Aisha's elder sister. He is every bit as useless and as aloof from the 'stream of time' as his unfortunate brother. Is there a flaw, a measure of double standards in the Mahfouzian time-morality? Far from it. The system is exemplarily fair and the fact of the matter is that Khadija redeems Ibrahim and his branch. Ugly, energetic, responsible, totally committed to her family and above all 'useful', she is a foil to her sister. Being the stronger party in the marriage, she imposes 'Jawwadism' in the heartland of 'Shawkatism' and she brings into the world two sons, Abd al-Mun'im and Ahmad, who are completely like her and unlike their father. She pulls her family back into 'the stream of time' and therefore survives and saves them.

There is another aspect to the relationship between time and man, namely the relationship between past and present, which transfers us from the realm of metaphysical time to that of value-impregnated time. In other words the past-present duality is about what man does with the life quota allocated him by metaphysical time. The life quota assigned to individual man is naturally finite and all too short for significant achievement, but that assigned to man socially or collectively (i.e. as a species) is infinite and carries equally infinite possibilities for improvement. It is the duty of each individual to use his share of time to the best of his ability towards this objective, i.e. the betterment of the human lot. This moral concept of time is central to Mahfouz's vision, as I have indicated before. It would be no exaggeration, indeed, to argue that the only source of hope in his work emanates from his view of man as a force endlessly active in a time continuum across individuals, generations, ages and cultures. Wherever he portrays man as an isolated human unit wrestling against the odds of time and space, the consequence is always tragic. 'Tragic' is indeed the word he uses to describe his view of life which ends in death for the individual. But, as we have seen, he stresses that while death is inevitable, it is incumbent on us (while we live) to fight social evils which are perfectly avoidable and which indirectly aid death in its perpetual victory over humanity. Now social evils can of course be remedied only in time. Not static time, but changing time. And change is about the tension between past and present – a tension whose arena extends from the soul of the individual to the full spectrum of society. This tension, of which we have seen various manifestations in previous works by the author, is much more profoundly explored in this novel.

The extension of *The Trilogy* across three generations provided the novelist with an excellent opportunity to explore this favourite theme of his through observing the mutation of values across generations, the time gap between different contemporaneous social classes, and the changing lifestyle concomitant with the changing value system. Through an intricate, multilayered, multi-directional symbolic system so well woven into the robustly realistic texture of the novel, Mahfouz renders the dichotomy that his nation still lives today. The generation of the parents stands for the past. The father, as mentioned before, is a bundle of contradictions: a stern, authoritarian, much-feared patriarch at home, but a cheerful, witty, much-loved friend and businessman outside; a true believer and pious worshipper in daytime, but at night a devoted libertine given to drink, women and merrymaking. Yet, all these contradictions live inside him in a harmony worthy only of a god. The phrase is actually Mahfouz's own comment on his character.[116] Nor should we think that he used the word 'god' lightly, for Abd al-Jawwad is portrayed as in every way a god in his home. This is not only shown through the supreme, unquestionable and irrevocable authority that he wields over the fates of the members of his household, and through episodes like the banishment of his wife from his home after 25 years of total obedience, for once going out without his permission (a banishment which evokes the Fall and expulsion from Heaven). Not only through this, but also the narrative prose which persistently attributes to him epithets and qualities appropriate to Allah. In this context we should perhaps call to the mind *al-Asma' al-husna* or the divine attributes of God in Islam whose contradictions are as wide as is the distance between 'the Merciful' and 'the Compassionate' on the one hand, and 'the Tyrant' and 'the Vengeful' on the other – compassion and tyranny both being attributes of Abd al-Jawwad, incidentally. This supreme harmony, this peaceful coexistence of opposites in the character of the father, is a masterly rendition of a culture at peace with itself, with neither external influence nor inner conflict. Needless to say, the father has little education beyond reading and writing and the basic book-keeping necessary for his trade. A merchant and the son of one, he was born in the old quarter of Jamaliyya and was to die in it. Practically intelligent, witty and socially accomplished, his ignorance of life beyond his small world is endearingly illustrated when he asks his son Kamal whether Charles Darwin (1809–82), about whom the latter had published an article in a newspaper, was a teacher at his school.[117] His generation represented the last bastion of the past in Egypt, the past when it reigned supreme, unchallenged and, like God, infallible. The harmony and freedom from conflict that he enjoyed is something that none of his children or their children will ever experience. Represented by Kamal in the second generation, and his nephews Ahmad and Abd al-Mun'im in the third, they are the ones to live through a duality of values, through the schizophrenia created by the encroachment of the present on the past and of the 'other' on the 'self'.

When, as an adult, Kamal discovers the duality of his father's nature, i.e. that the 'Divine' is also human, that 'God' can laugh and drink and play the tambourine as well as fornicate, the discovery shakes him to his foundations. It was as if his world had been deprived of the last gravitational force that held it in place. From that moment on his soul was to wander lost in the infinite space of doubt and disbelief. His father now is just 'another illusion',[118] no longer possessing 'the divine attributes that [his] bewitched eyes had seen in him in the past'.[119] At this point the symbolism almost comes up to the surface of the text as Kamal addresses his father in his mind with these words: 'But it is not you alone whose image has changed. God himself is no longer God as I worshipped Him in the past. I am sifting through His attributes to clean them from tyranny, despotism, coercion, dictatorship and the whole gamut of human instincts'.[120] Thus Kamal discards his veneration for his father in the same breath as he discards the conventional, religious image of God. In his drunken delirium, he condemns parenthood and the family, 'that hole in which stagnant water collects', and prays for 'a homeland without history and a life without past'.[121] The father dies, years after this revelation, following an air-raid that his frail heart could not withstand. Minutes before his death, Kamal had said by way of commenting on the effect of the air-raids on the old houses of Jamaliyya:

'If our houses are destroyed, they will at least have the honour of being destroyed by the latest devices of modern science'.[122] What is really destroyed is not the old houses, but the old values of their occupants. The death of the father as a result of an act of modern warfare is a symbolic ending for a symbolic character. He is the once-secure past ousted by Western modernity. His death in this manner is the forerunner of the death of another father/God figure and also at the hands of modern science, namely Gabalawi of the author's next novel, *Children of the Alley*.

Amina, the mother, is also an emblem of the past. The nuances of her portrait strengthen the symbolic dimension to her husband's, so that together they represent the past in its last secure days. Her relationship with her husband, characterised by total and unquestioning acceptance of his authority, is itself an image of the stability of the value system that frames this relationship. The imperturbable serenity of her temperament (much stressed by the author), like her husband's unique ability to accommodate his contradictions in a state of harmony, should be seen as another manifestation of the stability of the worldview behind it. By the time we reach the second generation, this stability is already shaken. This is conveyed by the completely different relationships that her daughters have with their husbands: in the case of Aisha a relationship of equality, and in the case of Khadija one where the woman has the upper hand. In the third generation the values of the old world become almost unrecognisable as one of the grand-children, Ahmad Shawkat, marries a working woman as much in contact with the reality outside the home as himself.

Illiterate, without any education except for an oral religious one steeped in superstition and received from her father (himself a man of religion), Amina is obviously the representative of a culture that at the beginning of the 20th century was not only almost totally religiously oriented, but happy to be so and unaware of an alternative. Like the culture she represents, she lived in complete isolation from the outside world, cocooned inside the *old* Cairo, or more accurately inside the walls of her home in old Cairo, where all she could see of the outside world was the view from the roof, which consisted of nothing but 'the minarets of mosques and the roofs of adjacent houses'.[123] She believed in the jinn and did all she could to placate those of their species that lived in her home. In the author's words, 'she knew much more about the world of the jinn than she did about that of humans'.[124] No wonder then that when, after 25 years of this protected, blindfolded life, she decides to venture out only as far as the al-Husayn Mosque in the immediate vicinity, the contact with outside reality is catastrophic in its consequences: she is hit by a car and has a broken collarbone which confines her to bed for three weeks. A yet more serious consequence was her temporary exile by her husband/God as a punishment for tasting of the forbidden tree-of-knowledge-of-the-extra-domestic. Just as the old Abd al-Jawwad's death, many years later, was to come as a consequence of the encounter with the devices of the modern world (i.e. the bombers conducting the air-raid), the meaning of the car that hits Amina should not be lost on us either. It too is a device of the modern world, its symbolic value heightened by its relative rarity on the streets of Cairo in those days.

The second volume of *The Trilogy*, *Palace of Desire*, is devoted to Kamal in his adolescence and early manhood. Some of the most profound soul-searching ever rendered in Arabic prose is contained in this volume. And it is written with such intensity and immediacy and with a poetic quality that must be drawn from the admitted autobiographical link between Kamal and his creator. As Mahfouz has often repeated, Kamal's spiritual crisis was that of an entire generation,[125] by which he meant his own. The crisis, as we have seen, consists in the now classic Mahfouzian conflict between old and new or past and present. Kamal's dilemma results from his exposure to an influence that his parents' generation did not experience. This was mainly the influence of modern Western thought disseminated through the modernisation of the educational system which had already taken root in the 1920s and 1930s when Kamal was growing up. The gap between the two generations is probably best dramatised in the book in the famous scene in which Kamal is taken to task by his awesome father for having published a newspaper article in which he expounded Darwin's theory of evolution. For the father the issue was crystal-clear: the Koran says that 'God made Adam of clay and that Adam was the father of mankind', and to publicize any views to the contrary was an act of denial of the faith. Kamal, however, was well past all that. Outwardly apologetic to his father, his inner thoughts ran like this: 'I will not open my heart again to myth and superstition ... Adam, my father! I have no father. Let my father be a monkey if Truth so wills.'[126]

Apart from scenes like the above, conversations with intellectual friends and an endless stream of internal monologues, Kamal's dilemma is delineated through two central relationships heightened by a symbolic dimension. The first is his relationship with his parents, already discussed; the second is his unrequited love for Aïda Shaddad. As we have seen, his relationship with his parents ends in his rejection of their symbolic value, i.e. as exponents of the past, even though he continues to love and respect them as parents. Aïda, on the other hand, represents the alternative value system and lifestyle that he craves but cannot quite attain. She is the elusive present which he cannot reach far enough to embrace, and her rejection of him is as symbolic as his of his parents.

Critics have tended to regard both Kamal's infatuation with Aïda and her rejection of him in terms of social class. This is undeniably one level on which the relationship can be perceived. Kamal is a commoner, the son of a small merchant who lives in the *old* popular area of Jamaliyya, whereas Aïda is the daughter of Abd al-Hamid Shaddad, wealthy aristocrat and friend of the exiled ex-Khedive of Egypt, who lives in a great mansion in the *new* Cairo suburb of Abbasiyya. The unwritten social code would permit Kamal to become Hussein Shaddad's (Aïda's brother) best friend, but marriage and the union of the families was a different matter altogether (not that Kamal ever went as far as proposing to Aïda, anyway).

Another level on which the relationship can be viewed, and which is in fact an upgrading of the class level, is the cultural one. Aïda, both personally and as a member of her class, does not belong to the traditional value system that Kamal and *his* class live by. She and *her* class are, or at least so appear to the bewildered and infatuated eyes of Kamal, emancipated from the past. To him she means modernity, European modernity with the full plethora of associations that the term brings. Throughout there is an insistence on her Parisian upbringing. Unlike his mother and sisters who never step out of the house (and if they do, it is from behind a *hijab* (veil) that they see the world), Aïda is a model of Parisian chicness who mixes freely with her brother's friends (including Kamal) while he watches and 'suffers the bewilderment of one steeped in the traditions of the Husayn Quarter'.[127] 'Has her breach of observed traditions brought scorn upon her in your eyes?' he says to himself. 'No. Rather, it has brought scorn upon observed traditions'.[128] And when he goes on a picnic to the Pyramids at Giza with Hussein, Aïda and their little sister Budur, he is shocked when they produce out of their lunch box ham sandwiches and beer, religiously forbidden food and drink that he has never tasted. Shocked as he is (as he also is when he discovers that Aïda knows more about Christianity and its ritual than about her own faith and that she attends mass at her French school and learns hymns off by heart while she cannot recite a single verse from the Koran), all this only serves to increase his fascination with her. This 'light attitude towards the prohibitions of religion', sanctified by her very embrace of them, would from now on, he fears, become necessary credentials for him to admire any woman in the future.[129] On that occasion he touches neither pork nor alcohol. Before long, however, his conversion completed, he would be taking pride in his atheism, announcing happily to his friends that he no longer prayed or kept the fast of Ramadan. Before long, too, he would be a customer at public bars and brothels: the process of his secularisation was accomplished.

Aïda is idolized by Kamal. He places her on a pedestal and worships her unconditionally and without hope of requital. In his fervid monologues he refers to her as *al-Maʿbud* (the worshipped one), and often alludes to her in words and phrases imbued with religious associations.[130] He sees her as pure spirit, is uncomfortable to see her eat and drink and unable to imagine her performing other biological functions or succumbing after marriage to such mortal changes as are brought about by pregnancy and childbirth. All this of course is in the eye of the beholder. Finally many facts are brought to the attention of the incredulous Kamal by a more down-to-earth friend. Aïda, three years Kamal's senior, more mature, experienced and sophisticated (as would be expected of a member of her class), is in reality as far as can be from Kamal's idealised image of her. She has been looking for a suitable match among her brother's friends and when she finds one she does not hesitate to use the unwitting Kamal to arouse his jealousy and urge him to move in the direction of marriage. She is cruel to her worshipper, carelessly hurting his feelings by mocking his rather large head and nose. Nor does she refrain from making his love for her a subject for ridicule in the family. Her realism is a foil to Kamal's romanticism, her materialism to his idealism, her maturity to his adolescence, her arrogance to his humility, her sense of purpose to his uncertainty, her exploitation to his devotion and her scorn to his love. With her qualities, both positive and negative, and with the nature of the unbalanced relationship between her and Kamal, she appears the perfect symbol of the ideal of modern Europe for whose sake Kamal's generation rejected the past without succeeding, however, in attaining it. The agonising situation is best summarised by the words of Riyad Qaldas, Kamal's friend, to him: 'You suggest to me the character of an Eastern man, torn between East and West, a man who has kept turning round himself until he became dizzy.'[131]

Kamal's infatuation with Aïda in his early youth is in my view not unrelated on the symbolic level to his infatuation with English soldiers as a child of some ten years. When the soldiers were stationed outside the family house during the revolution, Kamal is lured by their beauty: 'their blue eyes, gold hair and white skin'.[132] He becomes friends with them and every day on his way back from school, he would stop at their camp to have tea and to chat and sing with them. When the revolution is over and the soldiers evacuate the area, the child feels sorry for the end of the 'friendship which tied him to those superior masters who stood in his belief high above the rest of mankind'.[133] This obviously is an early manifestation of fascination with the 'other', that later will take the form of admiration for the 'beauty' of the culture of those soldiers rather than their good looks. It is, however, a love-hate relationship. During an anti-British demonstration that he is caught up in as an adult, Kamal is puzzled by his own attitude: 'In the morning my heart is inflamed with rebellion against the English, while at night the common spirit of human fellowship in pain calls for cooperation in the face of the riddle of man's destiny.'[134] What he is referring to is his

I dreamt of my mentor, Shaykh Mustafa Abd al-Raziq, when he was the head of al-Azhar. As he entered the main office, I rushed to catch up with him, offering my hand in greeting. Walking along with him, inside I saw a sprawling, spectacular garden. He told me that he had planted it himself – half with native roses, the other half with Western ones. He hoped the two would give birth to a wholly new kind – in form perfect, and in fragrance, sublime.

'Dream 180' from *Dreams of Departure*

nightly readings in Western thought. The parallelism between the childhood episode referred to above and the central story of his love for Aïda is not difficult to see: in both cases there is an innocent infatuation followed by a more mature disenchantment, though never a complete rejection. When in middle age Kamal walks in the funeral of Aïda without knowing, it seems a most cynical ending to a very romantic episode, all the more so because the 'goddess' of the past dies the second wife of an older man, having earlier been divorced by her aristocratic husband as well as made a pauper by her family's loss of fortune. What did Mahfouz want to say by that? Is it a tacit pronouncement on the sham of the old infatuation, on the depth of the chasm between inner illusion and outer reality? Or is it a pronouncement on the frailty of the alternative model? Or is it again just a lament over the vanity of human passion and the final mockery that Time has in store for the unwitting individual? The answer could be any, all, or none of these hypotheses; this very uncertainty being perhaps part of the enduring charm of this amazing love story.

Kamal's parents lived during the glorious, unassailable days of the past. By contrast, Kamal's time was one of tension between past and present, a tension which paralysed him and served to consume his energy in contemplating life rather than living and changing it. Hence his futile celibacy, his bewilderment, his endless hesitations, doubts and inaction. The third generation, as represented by Kamal's nephews Abd al-Mun'im and Ahmad, is however a generation of action. The two brothers are not internally torn between past and present like their uncle because the conflict is now externalised on the ground in society. Abd al-Mun'im, a Muslim Brother, believes that the solution for the troubles of individual and society lies in the return to the fundamentals of Islam: he is the past. Ahmad, on the other hand, sees the solution in the abandonment of old values and the adoption of science and socialism: he is the present. Both brothers are political activists taking risks for their separate causes and ending up in prison.

It is Ahmad, however, who has the sympathy of Kamal (and indeed the implicit sympathy of the novelist). I have argued earlier that Ahmad as a nationalist is an extension across time of Fahmy, who died prematurely in the struggle. Ahmad is also an improved version of Kamal; he is what Kamal could have been had he succeeded in freeing himself more radically from the past and from his romantic fixations. To prove the point, Mahfouz places Ahmad in a similar relationship to that which Kamal had with Aïda. His love too is directed towards the upper class, but his approach, unlike his uncle's, is daring and self-confident and when he meets with rejection, life does not stand still. His frustration is redirected towards a higher cause and is soon transcended.

The Trilogy, as we have seen, begins in 1917 and stops near the end of the Second World War, having been completed in 1952 shortly before Nasser's revolution. After the period of silence, discussed in the first chapter, which occupied the best part of the 1950s, Mahfouz spent most of the following two decades criticising the 1952 revolution and the new society it created – in much the same way as the novels of the 1940s had been dedicated to criticism of the old society. In 1982, however, 12 years after the death of Nasser, one year after Sadat's and 30 years into the life of a revolution that had long spent its force, it occurred to Mahfouz, perhaps feeling the additional weight of years and the national frustrations which came with them, to review and update, through another *roman fleuve*, Egypt's relationship with time and to examine again the sorrows inflicted by the public on the private. *There Only Remains an Hour* documents the political history of 20th-century Egypt from the time of the nationalist uprising against the British in 1919 down to the Camp David Accords and the Peace Treaty with Israel in 1979. It stops just short of the assassination of Sadat in 1981.

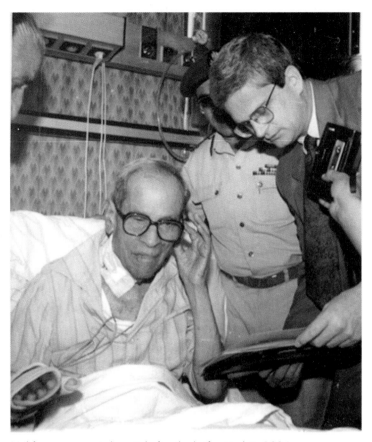

Mahfouz recovers in hospital after the knife attack in 1994

In *The Day the Leader was Killed* (1985), Mahfouz remains within the confines of his usual period, i.e. from 1919 to the time of writing, the period to which he was an eye-witness. The book is a short novella, the day of the title is 6 October 1981 and the leader killed is Anwar Sadat. The story is told through a number of alternating internal monologues divided among three characters, namely Muhtashimi (the grandfather), Alwan (his grandson) and Randa (the latter's fiancée). Despite its compactness, the book can be seen as yet another *roman fleuve*, looking at three generations, but mainly documenting the predicament of Egyptian youth during the Sadat era, and through parallelism between the consciousnesses of the old and the young creates the sense of a continuum of national frustration across generations.

Children of the Alley, serialised in *al-Ahram* newspaper in 1959 (though banned in book form in Egypt due to its contentious content for more than 40 years) was to mark Mahfouz's return to fiction writing after the sterile period which followed the completion of *The Trilogy*. To his native audience, it has by and large been seen as his most controversial novel because of its allegorical recasting of sacred religious figures. Different as it is both in subject matter and its episodic form from anything written before it, there is still a manner in which it can be seen, like its immediate predecessor, as a *roman fleuve*. The generations here, however, are those of the entire human family from Adam to modern man, and the time (totally external or public here, where there is no concern with personal tragedy) is the many millennia that it took humanity to grow out of belief in the supernatural into belief in science. Seen as such, the novel would readily present itself as a broadening of the spectrum of Kamal's spiritual journey in *The Trilogy* discussed above, and indeed as a universalisation of the theme of old and new or past and present, which Mahfouz harped on in all his preceding realistic fiction.

The novel is a panoramic view of the history of man and religion from the beginning of time to the present day. God, Satan, Adam, Moses, Jesus and Muhammad are all there, but without the halo of religious myth: the novel is an attempt at demythologizing humanity's religious quest. It begins with an episode which parallels the Koranic story of Adam's fall and his subsequent expulsion from Heaven, Heaven here being the 'Great House' of his father, Gabalawi (= God) with its vast garden. Adham, his son (= Adam) is banished to the *hara* (= the Earth) where he experiences toil and poverty after his happy life in the 'Great House'. Many years later when one of his two sons kills the other (in an episode allegorising the story of Cain and Abel), Gabalawi finally takes pity on his disconsolate son and as a token of forgiveness bequeaths his estate to his children and their posterity (= mankind) for ever and ever. Having done that, the old man retires inscrutably to his impregnable house on the border of the *hara* and is no more seen outside. The Trustee of the bequest (= the ruling class), however, soon turns into a thief who takes the income of the estate for himself and coerces the people of the *hara* through the employment of paid *futuwwas* or thugs. Thus social injustice began. But injustice engenders resistance; and this is exactly what Judaism, Christianity and Islam were all about according to Mahfouz. They are seen within the simplistic terms of the allegory as a succession of socio-political movements against a repressive system, aiming at establishing a just order on earth.

However, the successes of those prophets, or shall we say political rebels, were only of temporary duration, for each time the *hara* lapsed again into its old evil ways. Is there no hope then? 'Yes, there is,' comes the prophetic voice of the novelist in the fifth and last book of the novel. For there we encounter Arafa, the magician, who stands for modern science and inherits the role of social saviour, previously the prerogative of Gabalawi/God-inspired prophets. Indeed, the demise of the idea of God in the modern world is paralleled in the novel by the death of the old man Gabalawi (significantly instigated by the magician's clandestine raid on his forbidden house). The role of science as the modern world's god is spelt out by Arafa (note the meaningful choice of name from the Arabic root *'arafa,* 'to know') in a feverish and contrite speech after the death of the old man: 'A single word from *our* grandfather used to drive the good ones among his grandchildren to strive until death. His death should be stronger than his words. It makes it the duty of a good son to do everything, to take his place, to be him.'[135] Mahfouz goes even further in his endeavour to establish science as the legitimate heir of religion. This can be seen in the vision which Arafa has of a message left him by the dying old man and communicated by his maid. The text of the message is simply, 'Go to Arafa, the magician, and tell him on my authority that his grandfather died pleased with him'.[136] This immediately establishes Arafa as a recipient of revelation like his prophetic predecessors. What we have here is a gallant attempt by Mahfouz to bestow on science the spiritual power inherent in religion. On the other hand, the limitless potential of science to bring about the Benthamite dream of the 'greatest happiness for the greatest number' is emphasised when Arafa voices the hope that his magic 'may one day be able to destroy thugs, construct buildings, and provide for all the children of the quarter'.[137]

The novel ends on a pessimistic note with Arafa murdered at the hands of the Trustee and his *futuwwas*. Unlike the previous prophets, he leaves the *hara* worse off than it was before him. But amid the darkness there is a ray of hope: Arafa has left somewhere the notebook containing the secrets of his magic, and his brother and assistant Hanash, who survives the massacre, is going to find it and continue to work for the salvation of the *hara*, helped by its young, who begin to disappear mysteriously, creating the belief that they are running away to join Hanash in his endeavours and come back one day in force to set things right. Here as elsewhere Mahfouz puts his faith in the evolutionary movement of collective time. With *Children of the Alley*, Mahfouz closes one chapter in his literary career: his next novel was to herald a new phase in his writing.

Naguib Mahfouz, Nasser's Egypt and God

The Trilogy, as we have seen, was Mahfouz's last work written before the 1952 revolution, though first published under the new regime in 1956–7. The six novels beginning with *Khan al-Khalili* and culminating with *The Trilogy* were concerned to a large extent with a critical portrayal of Egyptian society and politics during the greater part of the first half of the 20th century. Foremost in the author's mind was the representation, on both the individual and social levels, of the tensions created by the conflict between past and present – the old traditional values and the new, Western-inspired ones. On the individual plane, Kamal Abd al-Jawwad's spiritual schism was perhaps the highest expression of that conflict. On the other hand, it was Kamal's two nephews, the fundamentalist Abd al-Mun'im and the socialist Ahmad, who gave that conflict its most forceful social expression.

After 1952 there was the creative gap, discussed earlier, which lasted until the serialised publication of *Children of the Alley* in 1959. The novelist tells us that in 1952 he had as many as seven plans for new novels waiting to be written with the lines of their plots *almost completed* and the portraits of their characters *crystallized.* The novels were to be a continuation of the trend which peaked with *The Trilogy.* The impulse to write, however, died and the plans were abandoned for ever.[138] During the heyday of the Nasser period, Mahfouz used to answer questions on 'the period of silence' in terms of the social and political reforms brought about by the revolution, which had rid society of the kind of issues which used to provoke him to write. In the more liberal post-Nasser era, however, he admitted that this explanation had been partly dictated by motives of self-protection against the wrath of the regime. He nevertheless remained unable to offer a satisfactory explanation in lieu of the discredited one.

Perhaps Mahfouz went too far in casting doubt on the motivation behind his initial explanation of his writer's block. The revolution brought about colossal changes in both the structure and government of Egyptian society and over a very short period at that. The result was that the society which had provided the novelist with his subject-matter for the previous decade or so virtually changed out of all recognition. He needed time to observe and absorb the new society with its different ills – or perhaps old ills in new dress. He also needed time to adapt his artist's tools to the new subject-matter. When these processes were completed he wrote *Children of the Alley* which, in spite of its ambitious religio-historical scope, appears to have been more concerned with modern Egyptian reality than its allegorical form readily betrays.

I only write when a split between society and me occurs ... I began to feel that the 1952 revolution which [at first] *had given me assurance and peace of mind was starting to go astray ... Many faults and errors upset me, especially the repression and the tortures and the imprisonments. Thus I began to write my big novel,* Children of the Alley, *which depicts the conflict between prophets and thugs ... I wanted to ask the revolutionary leaders which path they wanted to choose: the prophets' or the thugs'. The stories of the prophets provided an artistic framework, but my intention was to criticise the revolution and the existing social system. At that time I had noticed a new class evolving and growing extraordinarily rich. The question which then agonised me was whether we were moving towards socialism or towards feudalism of a new kind.*[139]

Mahfouz's condition for creativity (i.e. 'the split' between him and society) being in place within a few years of the revolution, his writing machine started to churn out works which embodied that split as created by Nasser's revolution. Nor was he to continue hiding behind the disguise of allegory as he had done in *Children of the Alley*. His next novel, *The Thief and the Dogs*, was to deal openly with the new realities of Egyptian society and so were all the novels of the 1960s. His approach to the new society was, however, to be made through the employment of fresh techniques, as if especially designed for it. The old keenness to describe at some length the physical and social environments and a certain way of life as seen in *The Trilogy* and earlier works was gone forever. Gone too were the multi-threaded plots, the immense variety of characters and the omniscient author's freedom to move at will among their consciousnesses. Instead, physical and social detail was now kept to the barest functional minimum. Plots were compact and the third-person narrative used, confining the viewpoint to the protagonist alone, whose mind was fully probed through the internal monologue technique, and through whose eyes all other characters and their actions were presented and judged. Above all, the language was to become much denser and more evocative than before, using image, motif and association to depict emotional tension and to hold together the entire fabric of the work. Most importantly on the thematic side, we will note a subsidence in the old preoccupation with the clash between cultural values. This was to give way to a concern with the tragic consequences of the clash between the individual and totalitarian authority – a perfectly understandable development in view of the political realities of the day. On the face of it the State adopted socialism and science and repressed into oblivion, for the time being, the Muslim fundamentalist trend, an active agent in the political arena during the two decades leading up to the revolution. Society now seemed, one must stress again, only on the face of it, to be proceeding harmoniously along modernist, largely secularised tracks. But all this was achieved artificially at the expense of its political emasculation and elimination of all dissent. Mahfouz was able to see from early on that it was not working, and could not work. When the regime faced its first real test in the 1967 war with Israel, the devastating result could not have taken by complete surprise any sensible decoder of signs in the novelist's output over the few preceding years.

Fittingly, *The Thief and the Dogs* (1961), the author's first link in the chain dealing directly with the shortcomings of the 1952 revolution, is about betrayal, mainly the betrayal of revolutionary ideals once power, with the privileges that come with it, is achieved. Thus the relationship between Said Mahran, the protagonist of the novel and the one betrayed,[140] and Rauf Ilwan, his fallen idol on whom he seeks to be avenged, is Mahfouz's metaphor for the rapid dissipation of the revolutionary ideal and his indictment of the newly emerged establishment which inherited all too soon the privileges and complacency of the *ancien regime*. Said Mahran, however, fails in achieving his objective. His bullets go astray, killing innocent people instead of their intended targets. Said, who nevertheless turns into a heroic symbol for the masses of the people, is hounded down by the entire apparatus of the State – the 'dogs' of the title. Said's failure is not of course without significance. The apparent moral is that true revolutionary action cannot originate in personal vendetta, nor is it a task for individuals on their own: organised action is essential, a view endorsed by Mahfouz himself who blamed his character for his lack of *the comprehensive outlook necessary for the revolutionary*, and for his preoccupation with only *those who betrayed him personally*. He went on to name this as *exactly the reason for his failure and death*.[141]

The Thief and the Dogs is not, however, a simple political parable – indeed none of the novels of the 1960s decade can be seen as just that. In all of them Mahfouz succeeded in transforming his probing of the predicament of the individual in his confrontation with authority into a consideration of such issues as the meaning of life, the value of human action and the alienation of the modern individual from both society and God – themes which led critics to associate the novelist's work during that period with the existentialist movement in Europe, particularly Camus and Sartre.[142] Thus Said's isolation and desperate loneliness are rendered in such terms as would make his story a powerful metaphor for the alienation of the nonconformist wherever he may be. Nor is his alienation only social, for in his obsession with setting right worldly reality he is unable to draw comfort from thoughts of the hereafter. This theme of modern man's alienation from God is introduced in the novel through the juxtaposition of Said's character with that of the old Sufi, Ali al-Junaydi. Homeless and hounded, with his soul devoured by the desire for revenge on those who wronged him, Said takes refuge momentarily in the house of Shaykh Junaydi, whom he has known since his childhood when he used to visit him with his father. Said and the Sufi shaykh are the emblems of two worlds that cannot meet: the mystic has achieved peace with the world by completely withdrawing from its harsh reality and creating an inner one for himself, while Said is too enmeshed in the ugliness of the world to be able to see or seek a way to deal with it other than by confrontation. *I reject any form of Sufism achieved at the expense of man's concern with the world and the life of people ... Sufi principles created by the Sufi to be applied to himself or to a superhuman group is no good for the rest of humanity.*[143]

One must remark here that the Sufi character introduced in *The Thief and the Dogs* for the first time appears to be Mahfouz's heightened replacement for the Muslim fundamentalist used in earlier novels. For one thing the latter had virtually disappeared from the visible social and political life of Nasser's Egypt so that it would have seemed anachronistic to allow it to play its traditional role in the author's work set in the post-revolutionary era. On the other hand, the Sufi figure with its symbolic potential must have appeared more appropriate to a novelist who was now more concerned with the metaphoric than the lifelike representation of reality.

In Mahfouz character is not fate – not altogether anyway. Nor is society. Although temperamental flaws and social injustice contribute in a major way to the defeat of his characters, his work often seems to point at something else that is wrong, something that lies at the very nature of things in the world – a contributory force that is indefinable and incomprehensible, but whose workings in our lives are undeniable. Otherwise, how can Said's stray bullets be explained? It happens twice: the first time when he tries to kill Ilish Sidra (his one-time lackey who betrayed him to the police and robbed him of his wife and money), and the second when he tries to kill Rauf Ilwan, his erstwhile political mentor who betrays their revolutionary ideals. On both occasions his bullets kill innocent victims. On the first occasion, when Said learns through the newspapers of the mistake, his thoughts run like this: 'What a waste of effort! I killed Shaban Husayn! Who are you Shaban? I did not know you and you did not know me. Did you have children? Did you imagine one day that a man you did not know … would kill you? Did you imagine that you would be killed for no reason? That you would be killed because Nabawiyya Sulayman married Ilish Sidra? That you would be killed in error, while Ilish and Nabawiyya and Rauf who ought to be killed would live on? And I, the killer, understand nothing. Not even Shaykh Ali al-Junaydi can understand this. I set out to solve part of the mystery only to unravel a deeper one.'[144]

Said's career of thievery could be explained in social terms (as the novel in fact tries to do through flashbacks to his boyhood), while his determination to punish his enemies at any cost could probably be understood in terms of a temperament too obsessive, impatient and perhaps idealistic to be able to channel its personal bitterness into constructive action. But how can the stray bullets be explained? It is society and character that lead Said to his perdition

– there is no doubt about that. But what is it which lays waste his effort and deprives his actions of meaning? In Said's own words, 'How absurd life would be if tomorrow I were to be executed for killing a man I did not know!'[145] A mechanical explanation is of course not unavailable. In the first instance Ilish Sidra had vacated the flat in anticipation of Said's intentions, so that when the latter shoots through the door in the dark, it is the new tenant he kills, while in the second instance it is the presence of an armed guard that takes Said by surprise, causing his hand to shake and his bullet to miss its intended target. But mechanical explanations by definition only explain the mechanics of a process or an occurrence – they do not explain the cause. Nor is there a cause that is explicable. The phenomenon, however, is not short of a name: fate (also known as coincidence or the interplay of space and time) – a key concept in Mahfouz's world-picture and a prime agent in the life of his characters, as established from his first novel, *Khufu's Wisdom*.

In his next novel, *Autumn Quail* (1962), Mahfouz pursues his examination of the relationship between the individual and authority, and again the theme of the corrupting influence of power over the one-time revolutionary.

The Search follows in 1964 with another metaphor of aborted dreams. Its protagonist's futile search for 'freedom, dignity and security' is no different from the national quest of modern Egyptians. But one must be careful not to read too much politics into this novel. In fact, of all the 1960s novels, this is the one with the least direct bearing on the political reality of the day. It is only in *The Search* that the above tripartite quest is transplanted from its habitual socio-political context to a metaphysical one. Thus Saber's search for his father on the realistic level is nothing short of mankind's search for metaphysical truth (or the Father who is in Heaven) on the symbolic level (the father as a symbol of God having already been used by Mahfouz in both *The Trilogy* and *Children of the Alley*).

But as Mahfouz's work has demonstrated before and since *The Search*, there is no metaphysical solution for man's problems on earth. 'Freedom, dignity and security' cannot come as a gift from heaven; they must be earned on earth. And they can be earned only through *work*. In lieu of God, Work (in the broad Sartrean sense of *engagement*) becomes the absolute value-giver – it is the only 'way' to the tripartite human ideal of 'freedom, dignity and security' (it is worth noting that the Arabic title of the novel is actually 'The Way', not 'The Search' as in the English translation). In the end Saber's search does not lead him to his father (physical or metaphysical) and in the futility and emptiness of the process he strays into crime, never losing hope as he awaits execution that his 'father' would find him and save him at the last moment.

The metaphysical search is carried on into Mahfouz's next novel, *The Beggar* (1965). The protagonist, Omar al-Hamzawi, a wealthy and successful lawyer and family man, is suddenly struck by existential *angst*. His work and family cease to mean anything to him and so does the rest of the universe. He is engulfed in a sense of the ultimate absurdity of all things. It all began when one day he teased a client of his on whose behalf he was fighting a case over the ownership of a plot of land: 'What if you were to win the case today and take possession of the land only for the government to come and seize it tomorrow?' Omar asks. 'Don't we live our life knowing full well that it is going to be taken away by God?' is the client's dismissive answer.[146] But it was an answer that Omar himself was never able to dismiss from his mind. Like Saber in the previous novel, he embarks on a long and arduous search for the ultimate truth. His search leads him along many dead ends, and close to madness.

Omar's spiritual crisis, while it is the central preoccupation of the book, is not set in a social vacuum, unlike the case with Saber in *The Search*: he is a former idealist and revolutionary who gave in to the comforts of material success and bourgeois living until the terrible emptiness of his life hit him out of the blue. Omar's meta-physical quest leads him eventually to the complete abnegation of society. He leaves family, friends and business and retires to a solitary cottage in the countryside, but eventually reality imposes itself on him and draws him back into the world. The ultimate truth then is *in* the world and not somewhere outside or beyond it. For Mahfouz any form of transcendental escapism is rejected.

The relentless search for meaning in life and the despair at its apparent absence continued to drive Mahfouz's imagination into the next novel, *Adrift on the Nile* (1966). Anis Zaki, the protagonist through whose consciousness we perceive the world of the novel, is a small middle-aged clerk in a government office (but also a well-read intellectual). He lost his wife and daughter 'to the same illness and in the same month', 20 years before the beginning of the novel's action;

In existentialist philosophy and in particular according to Jean-Paul Sartre (1905–80), *angst* is a kind of moral and metaphysical anguish, resulting from a state of heightened self-awareness. The energy generated by this awareness can help the *angst-stricken* individual drag himself out of despair and exercise his power of choice, thereby giving meaning to life. Sartre believes that man can emerge from his passive and indeterminate condition and by an act of will become *engagé;* whereupon he is committed (through *engagement*) to active participation in social and political life. Through commitment man provides a reason and a structure for his existence.[147]

he also had, for unspecified reasons, his hopes of a medical career quashed. Thus when we meet him, he is already accomplished in the art of living with life's frustrations and the sense of its meaninglessness. His answer to the harshness of social and existential reality is escape into an almost permanent narcotic stupor – a modified version within Mahfouz's world, one might say, of Omar's failed Sufi trances in *The Beggar.*

The novel is set almost entirely in a boathouse on the Nile in Cairo, where a group of men and women representing a cross-section of the well-to-do Egyptian middle class in the 1960s, including a lawyer, a journalist, an actor, a literary critic and a Foreign Office official, meet every night over hashish, drink and sex. They lead a totally self-indulgent and nihilistic kind of existence: inverted mysticism, one might say, or the abnegation of the soul rather than the senses, according to Mahfouz's value system. It is through Anis's endless stream of hashish-induced thoughts that the apathy, the purposelessness and the amorality of the group's life is placed in a historical and existential context. Here is one example: 'Had these friends met – as they do tonight – under a different guise in Roman times? And had they witnessed the fire of Rome? Why did the moon split from the earth pulling up the mountains? And which one was it of the French Revolution's men who was killed in the bathroom by the hand of a beautiful woman? And how many of his contemporaries died of chronic constipation?'[148] Through this string of freely associated ideas (and scores more like it) Anis's tragedy and by proxy that of his boathouse companions is shown as part of a human condition controlled by an absurdity and a randomness that has always lain at the heart of existence. Needless to say Anis's wildest narcotic fantasies are the product of his author's most sober contemplative moments, their incoherence therefore deceptive. Thus the ancient Roman depravity is only recalled to underline current depravity. On the one hand the painful irony inherent in the undignified death of Jean-Paul Marat (1743–93) (a leader of a revolution which changed the course of human history) is all too obvious. But the ultimate absurdity lies in the next thought: if death is the inevitable end for all, what difference does it make to be a Marat or a nobody; to be assassinated or to die of chronic constipation? The ultimate human indignity is death; the rest is a matter of detail. Finally, with the image of the moon separating from the earth and pulling the mountains up, the absurdity of human life and history is placed in the context of the infinite absurdity at the centre of the universe.

Against cosmic and historic absurdity are shown the social absurdities of Egypt in the 1960s where 'everyone is writing about socialism, while most dream about wealth'.[149] In one of Anis's flights into history which Mahfouz uses for what then was dangerously obvious political projection, Anis calls up an ancient Egyptian sage and asks him to repeat the song he used to sing for Pharaoh. The song runs like this:

Your companions have lied to you:
These are years of war and hardship.[150]
What has become of Egypt? –
The Nile still brings along its flood.
Wealthy now is he who naught had before.[151] Would that I
    spoke up then!
Wise, perceptive and just are you,
But you let corruption feed on the land. Behold how your
    commands are scorned! When would you graciously
    desire
That someone come and tell you the truth?[152]

No fantasy of hashish stupor this and no song by an ancient sage to an ancient pharaoh, but the supplication of a modern sage to a modern pharaoh. This was Mahfouz's prophetic plea to Nasser on the eve of 1967.

As always in Mahfouz, any form of escapism, isolationism or withdrawal from society is doomed to failure – reality always imposes itself in the end on those who run away from it. One night the boathouse companions decided to celebrate a public holiday by breaking their routine and going out for a midnight drive in the desert, south of Cairo. They cram themselves into the car of the actor, who drives at a crazy speed killing a peasant on the road. With the tacit agreement of the others, he fails to stop or report the accident. They all meet again at the boathouse on the following evening. But they are now a restless, frightened, conscience-stricken and mutually recriminating lot. The accident has shattered all their illusions and forced them out of their escapist stupor into the harshness of reality. The novel ends very pessimistically in that none of the characters is able to muster enough moral courage to report the accident and bear his or her share of responsibility for it. In retrospect it is not difficult to understand the extent of the author's melancholy inasmuch as it is difficult not to see the boathouse as symbolic of a society on the verge of sinking, and the car accident in terms of an oracular vision pointing at the other catastrophic accident then awaiting the nation round the corner of history – the 1967 defeat in the war with Israel.

On the publication of *Adrift on the Nile*, Abd al-Hakim 'Amir, the then Commander-in-Chief of the armed forces and Vice-President, said to Nasser, 'He [Mahfouz] has gone over the top and must be taught a lesson.' Nasser then consulted with his minister of culture, Tharwat 'Ukasha, who advised as follows: 'Mr President, in all honesty I tell you that if art could not enjoy this [little] margin of freedom, it would cease to be art.' 'Point taken; consider the matter closed!' answered Nasser calmly.[153]

Pessimistic as the author's vision is on the immediate level of meaning, he appears, however, to preserve his faith (maybe in a tongue-in-cheek manner) on the anthropological or evolutionary plane. The book ends with Anis again soaring to narcotic heights and thinking along these lines: 'The origin of all trouble was the skill of a monkey, who learned to walk upright, thereby freeing his hands. He came down from the tree-top monkey paradise to the ground of the forest. They told him to climb back up before the beasts got him. But in one hand he grasped a tree branch and in the other a stone and went cautiously on, looking ahead towards an endless road.'[154] What optimism is latent in these closing lines of the novel draws of course from Mahfouz's belief in collective human time, time as 'the evolutionary spirit of man'.

As if exhausted by the metaphysical search which spanned the last three novels, Mahfouz drops it altogether in *Miramar* (1967). The socio-political concern which infiltrated at a steadily increasing rate all three metaphysical novels swells up in *Miramar* to shut out every other concern. The novel was also technically innovative within the framework of Mahfouz's output up to that point. The events of the story are told in the first person by four of the main characters, readers thereby made privy to each character's judgement of the others instead of being limited to the viewpoint of only one character as has been the case since *The Thief and the Dogs*. It was not Mahfouz, however, who pioneered this technique in the Egyptian novel; a younger Egyptian novelist, Fathi Ghanem (1924–99), had already published in 1962 his quartet *The Man who Lost his Shadow*.[155] Rather than marking a turning-point in technique, *Miramar* actually marked a shift of interest from contemplating the human condition in its timeless and universal aspects to a more mundane contemplation of the immediate manifestations of this condition in Egyptian socio-political reality. This new phase was to maintain its grip on Mahfouz until the mid-1970s, as we shall see.

Miramar was Mahfouz's last *cri de coeur* against the aberrations of the 1952 revolution before the 1967 debacle. As in *Adrift on the Nile*, it puts together a group of different people in a confined space (the *pension* Miramar here substitutes the boathouse there) and allows the frictions arising from conflicts of temperaments and interests to escalate to a tragic climax. Each of the patrons of the *pension* represents a section of the contemporary society of Egypt with Zohra, the peasant maidservant, standing for Egypt. Significantly, the most abhorrently depicted character is Sarhan al-Beheiry, the representative of the lower middle class, the class empowered by the revolution to inherit the office and authority of the ousted aristocracy and upper middle class. Torn between an insatiable lust for life on the one hand, and meagre means on the other, Sarhan betrays, like his progenitor Rauf Ilwan in *The Thief and the Dogs*, the principles of the revolution he never ceases to pay lip service to. His moral bankruptcy and eventual suicide indicate Mahfouz's condemnation of the revolution's failure to lead by example. Written on the eve of Egypt's shattering defeat in 1967, events were soon to justify the sombreness of Mahfouz's mood!

What the oracle saw in *Adrift on the Nile* and *Miramar* came to pass on 5 June 1967. The shock kept Mahfouz from writing novels for nearly five years (between 1961 and 1967 he had published one novel every year, 1963 excepted). It may be that the mood of despondency and distraction that swept the intelligentsia and the rest of the country in the aftermath of the defeat left him in no frame of mind for the elaborate, lengthy structures that novels are. His creativity, however, found a way out in an outburst of short-story writing – in the three years from 1969 to 1971 he published four collections. It was in 1972 that *Mirrors*, his first novel since *Miramar,* was published, followed in rapid succession by *Love in the Rain* (1973) and *Karnak Café* (1974).

Mirrors was a panoramic view of Egyptian society from around the beginning of the century to the time of writing, consisting of 55 character sketches based on people that Mahfouz knew at different stages of his life. They represent a cross-section of Egyptian society over a number of generations. About one-quarter of the portraits are of women and through their stories the history of female emancipation in Egypt is related and also that of changing sexual morality. In evidence also is the usual intellectual Mahfouziana: religion, science, socialism, art, philosophy, society and the individual, etc. The book is a heap of images, broken in the flux of time, each a fragment of human flotsam carried forward by the eternal current. Perhaps in the very fragmentariness of the novel is its unity. It was also in some of its episodes that Mahfouz tried for the first time in his fiction to explore the mood of the nation after the defeat. Issues like the torture of political prisoners, the increasing emigration from the country of its despairing best youth, and the gradual collapse of moral ideals were briefly touched upon here, to be picked up again and elaborated in *Love in the Rain* and *Karnak Café*. Together the two novels evoke the national sense of loss and humiliation at the defeat, the irreparable damage to the dignity of the individual following years of repression of real and imaginary opponents, and the public apathy to events, engendered by the people's lack of trust in the regime and the habits of long years of being led from above without any measure of democratic participation in the government of their country. Inevitably these novels (both published after Nasser's death) are more candid in their criticisms, often dealing directly with issues which would have been too dangerous to address in the 1960s. Both novels are of a documentary nature, dealing with issues topical at the time of writing and seem rather dated today, and are artistically negligible in themselves. Posterity, however, will certainly treasure them as priceless sources for the social and political history of their time. Mahfouz himself seemed aware of the shortcomings of these works when he argued in the course of commenting on *Karnak Café*: *I am prepared to write a novel ... to support a view which I respect, or in order to make a personal comment on certain political circumstances, even if such a novel was destined to die as soon as the occasion for which it was written had elapsed.*[156]

After three novels and many more short stories which dealt partly or wholly, directly or indirectly, with both the germination and the aftermath of 1967, and after a long exile in modern Cairo and in Alexandria, apparently too weary and too nostalgic, Mahfouz gave in again unconditionally to the combined charms of his old Jamaliyya and metaphysics. The homecoming was marked by *Fountain and Tomb* (to be discussed in the next chapter), *Respected Sir*, and *Heart of the Night* (all three published in 1975).

The author's lifelong metaphysical anguish, suppressed under immense socio-political pressure since *Adrift on the Nile*, is allowed to breathe again in *Heart of the Night*, which is nothing but a condensed allegory of the spiritual evolution of mankind. Since this was well-trodden ground for Mahfouz, it is no surprise that he found it convenient to borrow some of the symbols he had already used in his earlier allegory on the same subject, i.e. *Children of the Alley*. So here too we have a rich and powerful God-like father living in near-seclusion in a fortress of a house standing in the middle of a paradise of a garden surrounded by high impenetrable walls. The man is a curious mixture of kindness and ruthlessness. The kindness is boundless as long as his descendants tacitly surrender their freedom of choice to him. Otherwise, he turns ruthless, as happens when Sayyid al-Rawi (alias Gabalawi!) banishes from his house and mercy to destitute life and premature death his only-begotten son for marrying against his wishes. The rest of the story continues with an allegorisation of the trials of man on earth, the dichotomy of pride in human *experience* and the hankering for the lost *innocence* of prelapsian existence etc. If it is valid to argue that *The Search* and *The Beggar* represent modern man's remorseful quest for the God he has lost or wasted on the way to civilisation, then it may be likewise valid to argue that *Heart of the Night* is the author's endeavour to retrace the course of the original journey, i.e. the flight from God. And 'flight' is indeed an appropriate word to describe the situation, for the story of the Original Sin as Mahfouz pictures it may have been an expulsion or banishment from God's point of view, but from the human point of view it was also a wilful act of escape, a conscious preference for the trials of freedom over the security of bondage – it was a mutual act of rejection between an obstinate maker and a creature too much in his image.

Heart of the Night is a thesis novel shot through and through with transparent symbolism. It is a work rich in thought and vision, which have not been successfully transformed into artistic metaphor – it teaches more than it delights. Much more successful as a work of art is the simultaneously published *Respected Sir*, set in Mahfouz's familiar terrain of government departments. The novel uses the ambition of a minor clerk in a government office to rise to the sublime rank of director-general as a metaphor for man's quest for the divine. The two-tier poetic narration works perfectly on both realistic and symbolic levels in this masterly little novel.

Five years later, Mahfouz appeared still preoccupied with metaphors of the metaphysical quest. *The Age of Love* (1980) was nothing more than a repetitive recasting of *Heart of the Night*: another simple allegory about the rebellious flight from God, followed by a remorseful and painful return. The thesis and metaphor are the same, while the language sorely lacks the poetic quality we have come to expect of Mahfouz as a matter of course. *The Age of Love* bears all the marks of a work composed at a moment when the author's creativity was at a low ebb.

A Form My Own: The Episodic Novels

Arabic literature, both classical and popular, has always abounded in forms of prose narrative. In the classical tradition, one can cite works like *Ayyam al-'arab* (the Battle-Days of the Arabs); the 8th-century animal fables of *Kalila and Dimna* (derived through Pahlavi from the Sanskrit *Fables of Bidpai* or *The Pnchatantra*) which Ibn al-Muqaffa' translated from Pahlavi; and the *maqamat*, or pica-resque adventures in rhymed prose, written by al-Hamadhani (967–1007) and al-Hariri (1054–1122). In the popular tradition, on the other hand, there was *The Thousand and One Nights* (also known as *The Arabian Nights*) and the many medieval works of *sira* (epic accounts of heroic exploits) such as *Sirat Bani Hilal* and *Sirat 'Antar,* to name but two. The above works are very different literary expressions composed over a period of many centuries; some are classical compositions, others are folk works of oral origin; some were written by known authors at a particular time, others composed by anonymous ones over many generations and across several countries. There is, however, one element which is common to all of them: their episodic structure. Some of these works, like *Kalila and Dimna* and *The Arabian Nights*, have their semi-independent episodes held together by a frame story, while others, such as the *maqamat*, enjoy no more semblance of unity than the fact that all the episodes or adventures figure the same picaroon or rogue as hero, otherwise being virtually independ-ent of each other. Evidently none of these Arabic narrative forms conforms to the traditional Western definition of plot as laid down by Aristotle (384–322 BC) in his *Poetics*, and which has largely governed the structure of the Western novel since its evolution and until fairly recently. In the late 19th and early 20th centuries, during the nascent days of modern Arabic fiction, attempts were made to revive, and adapt to the modes of the modern Arabic language and contemporary society, one of these indigenous narrative forms, namely the *maqama*. Those attempts proved, however, out of step with the times and were quickly ousted by the growing trend to evolve modes of fiction in Arabic along the lines of Western tradition.

Thus when Mahfouz arrived on the scene in the late 1930s, the novel as a literary genre cast in a borrowed Western mould had already entered the body of Arabic creative writing. Much of the story of Mahfouz's enormous contribution in developing this genre to full maturity, and adapting to his purposes and pushing to the limit, stage by stage, the potentials of his so-called borrowed mould, has already been told in the course of this book. One chapter of the story remains, however: the account of his own rebellion against the mould he had spent so much of his creative life in mastering and perfecting. As early as 1966, at the height of his absorption in the techniques of modernism, Mahfouz had boldly argued: *It is quite possible that I should come across a subject for which no form would be good enough except the* maqama; *in which case I will write my novel in the* maqama *style regardless.*[157] With the benefit of hindsight, this was an outburst by an adventurous and self-confident spirit rather than a declaration of intent – Mahfouz never came to write anything in the *maqama* form. He was, however, to create an episodic mould of his own and pour into it some of the most astounding achievements of his creative imagination, such as *The Harafish* and *Arabian Nights and Days*. It was from the early 1970s onwards that Mahfouz tended increasingly to express himself in the episodic mode (though not to the exclusion of the familiar Western form, which he continued to use sporadically).

The episodic phase begins tentatively with the 55 nostalgic character sketches of *Mirrors* in 1972, discussed in the previous chapter, and the 78 quasi-autobiographical tales of *Fountain and Tomb* in 1975. It would appear that the author was here in the business of using fragments of his life and times as the training ground for his new form. His success in transforming life matter into art and imposing order and meaning on those fragments must have strengthened his conviction that the new form was going to work. When, two years later, he published *Harafish* (a novel which today would appear on any shortlist of his most enduring achievements), it was immediately clear that the master craftsman had pushed his newly discovered form to the limits of its potential. The enterprise which commenced with character vignettes and recollections of childhood in the first two works was extended in *Harafish* in ten lengthy tales which together evoked the human condition from creation to a millenarian future. Mahfouz summed up his experiment with the new form in these terms: *When I started writing novels, I used to think that the European form of the novel was sacred. But as you grow older, your outlook changes; you want to free yourself from all that has been imposed on you, albeit in a natural and spontaneous way, and not just to break rules and be different. You find yourself searching for a* [certain] *tune deep down ... As if you were saying to yourself: 'Those forms which* [the Europeans] *wrote in – were they not artistic moulds that they created? Why can't I create a mould of my own?' ... But I must make clear one important point: imitating the old* [i.e. Arabic traditional forms] *is no different from imitating the new* [i.e. European form]; *both are acts of bondage.*[158]

Has Mahfouz indeed created 'a mould of his own' in these episodic works? My own feeling is that he has, but only in the sense that the author's imagination was the melting-pot in which the 'old' and the 'new' were fused together to produce 'his own mould'. There is no doubt in my mind that the originality of the episodic phase would not have been possible without the novelist's long experience in the arts of Western modernism, traces of whose modes of expression as well as sensibility are no less recognisable in the episodic works than are some of the qualities of the indigenous arts of storytelling. In the last analysis, it is a tribute to the author's accomplishment that the end-product can only be described as Mahfouzian.

The last episode of *Mirrors'* character sketches, told in evocative prose, portrays a female figure from the narrator's early childhood and is set in Jamaliyya, Mahfouz's birthplace in old Cairo. It tells of the child-narrator's fascination with a teenage girl living across the street. It ends with the little boy united after many failed attempts with his enchantress. She seats him on a sofa in her room and entertains him by reading his fortune for him: 'She began to trace the lines on the palm of my hand and read the future, but I was absorbed with the whole of my consciousness in her beautiful face'.[159]

This last episode of *Mirrors* could have been the first of *Fountain and Tomb* (1975). Published three years after *Mirrors*, it proved at the time that the new episodic form introduced in *Mirrors* was there to stay. It too is made up of 78 episodes. Each is called a *hikaya* (tale) and given a serial number; *hikaya* being a term associated with popular traditional narrative forms in Arabic. *Fountain and Tomb* carries on from where *Mirrors* broke off: the journey into the narrator's childhood continues – the narrator here not distinguished from Mahfouz who has acknowledged that the work reflects his own childhood.[160] Jamaliyya is evoked powerfully and poetically in this work, and it is here that Mahfouz's symbolic repertoire of the *hara*, the *takiyya*, the *qabw* and the *futuwwa* is born. The book is about private time rather than public time, and for once Mahfouz has written a work of reminiscences which does not get enmeshed in the politics of Egypt. The revolution of 1919 is there of course but only from the viewpoint of a child and as one

Mahfouz reading the newspaper in the Ali Baba café

of many factors contributing to the growth of his awareness. It is
there only as are accounts of his circumcision, first days at school,
childhood love and budding sexuality, the first encounter with
death, etc: the book is largely a *bildungsroman* of sorts, and Mahfouz
pronounced it the most autobiographical of his novels.[161]

Episodic as the novel is, there is yet another way in which a
sense of unity can be seen in its fragments. The book opens with a
tale recounting a mystical experience which the child undergoes.
One day, tired of playing, he dozes off in front of the wall of the
old *takiyya*, that dervish house (much like a monastery) standing
aloof in the *hara*, beset with mystery, its gates and windows always
shut and strange hymns occasionally wafting up from its garden.
When the child comes to, late in the afternoon, he feels himself
close to a gentle presence. He looks towards the *takiyya* and under

the mulberry tree he sees a dervish standing: 'but not like those I have seen before. He was very old and very tall, his face a shining pool of light. His cloak was green and his high turban white. He was magnificent beyond description or imagination. I looked at him so intently until I became intoxicated with the light that radiated from him and I felt his presence fill the universe. A sweet thought told me that he was the owner of the place and the one in charge.'[162]

The child tells the dervish that he loves mulberries, but all he gets by way of reply is an incantation in a foreign tongue. The dervish then throws him a mulberry. Or so the boy imagines, for when he kneels to pick it up he finds nothing. When he stands up again, the dervish has disappeared and darkness fallen. When the boy tells the story to his father, he is reluctant to believe it as the great dervish has never been known to leave his cloister. Later in his life, the child, now an adult, keeps wondering whether he really saw the great dervish or just imagined it, and if it were true why he had never appeared again: 'Thus I had created a myth and then shattered it. Nevertheless the alleged vision has sunk deep in my soul, a memory so sweet. Furthermore, I am still mad about mulberries.'[163]

The child's vision of the great dervish is of course symbolic of mankind's vision of God, just as the inscrutable *takiyya* with its garden and craved-for mulberry trees stands for Heaven, just as Gabalawi's mansion and garden did before in *Children of the Alley*. The *takiyya* is used as an occasional leitmotif in the book, always associated with light and peace in contrast with another motif, the *qabw* or vault, which is associated with darkness and where evil spirits live and heinous crimes are perpetrated. The experience of the first tale is recapitulated in the last where the child, now a little more mature, discusses his vision with a knowledgeable friend of his father's who had himself once been obsessed with the riddle of the *takiyya*. The conversation only serves to reaffirm the child's doubts and incomprehension. Significantly, however, he stresses that, in spite of everything, he 'cannot imagine a *takiyya* without a Great Dervish'.[164] The two tales about the *takiyya*, one beginning the book and the other ending it, seem to encircle, with their associations of the eternal, all the other tales that occur between them, thereby giving the novel a measure of formal unity. It is as if the encircled tales were instances of the temporal taking place within the framework of the eternal.

Within two years of *Fountain and Tomb*, Mahfouz was to publish another novel in the episodic mould and one of truly epic dimensions, *The Harafish*, an accomplished re-rendering of *Children of the Alley*.

The locale is the same (the *hara*); the power structure is the same (a pact between the rich and the *futuwwas* to plunder the rights of Gabalawi's children, the *harafish*); attempts to break the power structure are also the same (strong, good individuals establish short-lived justice before the old evil pattern is restored). *Harafish* is thus in essence Gabalawi's *hara* revisited. It is a fresh attempt by the author to answer in the broadest possible terms the agonising question: why does social evil exist and how can it be eradicated? To this newer attempt Mahfouz has brought the wealth of technical and stylistic expertise accumulated since the earlier one. The result is a much more mature work. Rather than creating an allegory in

Sources define a *harfush* (singular of *harafish*) variously as a member of the lower classes, a person of bad character, a ruffian, a scamp, etc. Mahfouz, however, uses the term loosely to refer to the deprived and oppressed classes of society. In using the word *harafish* and making them the protagonists of his novel, Mahfouz was modernising and endowing with a new vision a well-established popular narrative form whose tradition includes parts of *The Arabian Nights* and the famous popular *siras* (heroic exploits). Historical sources which chronicle the uprisings and practices of *harafish* in Cairo during the Mameluke period are numerous and Mahfouz is almost certain to have read some of them.

which existing religious myth is deflated, the novelist here creates his own myth out of a very familiar reality. Thus while *Children of the Alley* would be terribly impoverished if read without reference to its preconceived religio-mythological framework (the Bible and the Koran), *Harafish* is a self-contained work whose meaning stems solely from the sum of its parts.

Like *Children of the Alley*, *Harafish*, in its own way, is a *roman fleuve*. It is so, however, in a much looser sense of the term than we mean when we apply it for instance to *The Trilogy*. The novel is made up of ten tales which span the history of some 16 generations of the Nagis, descendants of the great Ashur al-Nagi, founder of the family. The *hara* where the action of the novel takes place is located in Mahfouz's familiar terrain in old Cairo without naming real places or defining period. The number of generations involved in the ten tales of the book would, on the other hand, easily suggest a time span of several centuries. Mahfouz in fact deliberately isolates the *hara* of the *harafish* from any specific framework of reference in locale or time. This device, coupled with a dense, evocative prose style which persistently infuses a subtle symbolism into such features of the *hara* as the *takiyya*, the *qabw*, the adjacent *khala'* and the giant minaret without a mosque, universalizes the *hara* into a timeless image of the human condition as the novelist perceives it (see the first chapter for the meanings of these terms).

In the beginning was Ashur, who later came to be called al-Nagi (the Survivor) because he was the only man to survive the plague which struck the *hara*. And Ashur was an illegitimate child abandoned in the dead of the night near the wall of the *takiyya* where he was picked up and adopted by Shaykh Afra Zaydan, an old, good-hearted, blind man with a sterile wife. In their care the child grows into a strong giant of a man with an innocent soul and a kind heart. From his young days 'his heart opened up to the joy and the light and the songs [of the *takiyya*]'.[165]

Ashur was content with his life and 'he thought that he would remain in paradise until the end',[166] but the old man dies and the old woman is forced to return to her native village. Thus Ashur finds himself alone in the empty *khala'*, well out of paradise, 'but a voice rising from his heart's depth told him that though the earth may seem empty, it is filled with the mercy of the Compassionate One'.[167] Ashur, however, was not quite alone on earth, for there was Darwish, Shaykh Afra's younger brother, who was brought up in the same house with Ashur. But he is an evil bandit who, after the death of his godly brother, tries to recruit Ashur's enormous strength in the service of crime. Ashur, however, will not be corrupted and as each goes his own way, Darwish throws in Ashur's face the stigma that has been kept from him for many years: that he was a bastard, a child of sin. In his despair Ashur is drawn to the *takiyya* with its trees, birds, green lawns and singing dervishes: 'The gate beckons to him. And in his heart he hears a whisper: Knock! Ask permission! Enter! Yours will be the grace and the peace and the joy. Turn into a mulberry tree. Let the sweet nectar fill you! Let your leaves nourish the silkworms. In the end hands that are pure will pick you in exultation.' But when he calls on the dervishes to offer his services: 'They hide away. They give no answer. Even the sparrows eye him with suspicion. They do not speak his language and he does not speak theirs. The stream runs no more and the grass halts its dance – no one needs his services.'[168] Rejected by the *takiyya,* and left alone with evil in the *hara*, Ashur learns that he will have to fight for survival (on earth) single-handedly. Mahfouz has told the story of Adam again (compare Adham in *Children of the Alley*). But while this account stands on its own merits, gaining in profundity as we gradually discover its remoter echoes, the earlier one serves mainly as a code for the Koranic story, and as we decipher it, it ceases to interest us except in so far as we want to see the extent to which it follows or deviates from the original.

Ashur obtains a job in the *hara* as a cart-driver. His devotion and honesty recommend him to his employer, who gives him his daughter in marriage. He begets three sons with her. But he never loses his attachment to the *takiyya*, opposite which he would always sit in the evenings listening to the dervishes' inscrutable songs and thinking about the wrongful ways of men and the frailties of the soul. He sees much that is unjust in the *hara* but his strength remains an unused potential to set it right. Then Darwish, who had been serving a prison sentence, is released and returns to the *hara* where he starts a bar-cum-brothel. To Ashur's consternation, his own sons soon become patrons of the evil place. He falls out with them and they run away from home. Soon, however, it transpires that Ashur himself is not immune to temptation and weakness of the flesh. He falls for Fulla, barmaid-cum-whore at Darwish's place. To the shock of his family and the whole *hara* he takes her as his second wife. Ashur's full humanity is thus emphasised in spite of the obvious saintly dimension to his character. Emphasised too is the entwined nature of good and evil. Fulla, however, is reformed by marriage and she bears him another son, Shams al-Din. For a while Ashur is a happy and contented man.

Then the plague strikes the *hara* and death goes on the rampage, sparing neither rich nor poor. Ashur is frightened and he sees it as the wrath of God. He sees a vision in a dream of his adoptive father Shaykh Afra leading him out of the *hara* into the mountains and the surrounding *khala'*. He decides to act on the vision. He invites his first wife and his sons by her to accompany him but they refuse and so do the people of the *hara* who accuse him of madness. Thus only Ashur, Fulla and their baby son Shams al-Din move with their donkey, cart and provisions to the desert, out of reach of death's ravages. They stay there for six months in total seclusion. In the *khala'* there is ample time for Ashur to worship and to meditate. He sees his *hara* 'as a jewel sunk in mud', and discovers that 'he loves it even with its shortcomings'. But he also comes to believe that 'mankind deserves what it suffers'. However, he does not lose his optimism and feels that 'he is being born anew'.[169] Eventually they return to a *hara* which is now as deserted as the emptiness they have returned from: the plague has washed it clean of life. Only the *takiyya* remains intact and the singing still wafts over its impregnable walls. Mahfouz has expropriated the story of Noah and the Ark with admirable sleight of hand, augmenting the symbolic value of Ashur (who encompasses both Adam and Noah) and greatly enhancing the sense of timelessness necessary for his myth-creating task.

Ashur and his family resettle then in what is virtually a ghost *hara*. One day Ashur succumbs to the temptation of walking into what used to be the mansion of the wealthiest family in the *hara*. The riches he sees stun him. They decide to abandon their basement room to live in the deserted palace. Ashur silences his pangs of conscience by arguing to himself that the house is without an owner and that wealth is legitimate as long as it is legitimately spent.[170] Gradually life starts to come back to the *hara*, with only the houses of the rich remaining vacant. When the *harafish* start to re-inhabit the *hara*, Ashur is already established in his new palace. He begins to spend lavishly on the poor from his newly-acquired wealth until there is no one left without a job or a small business. He also has the *hara* cleaned up, builds a small mosque, a drinking fountain and a donkey trough. Thus Ashur becomes the undisputed master of the *hara*. The *harafish*, having never known a rich man who behaved in that manner, call him a saint and argue that it was for that reason that God saved him alone from the plague. Thus wealth is redistributed fairly in the post-epidemic *hara* (or post-diluvian world) and human society appears for a while to be at peace with itself.

Before long, however, the government recovers from the aftermath of the epidemic and begins to take stock of the properties and estates of the dead. When Ashur is unable to produce proof of ownership, the estate is seized and he goes to prison, the uncrowned hero, nevertheless, of the *hara*'s poor. During his absence, Darwish takes control of the *hara* as *futuwwa* and a reign of terror begins for the benefit of the rich and at the expense of the *harafish.* No wonder then when Ashur is released from jail, they give him a hero's welcome, while Darwish's gang disappears into thin air. Thus Ashur finds himself the unrivalled *futuwwa* of the *hara.* The following extract is the closing paragraph of the story of Ashur al-Nagi, the first tale of *Harafish.* It sums up clearly the essence of what Mahfouz believed good government should be founded upon: 'As the *harafish* expected, Ashur established his *fatwana* [strongman's rule] on principles hitherto unknown. He went back to his original job [as cart-driver] and basement flat. He also obliged his men to earn their living by the sweat of their brow, thereby stamping out *baltaga* [living off other people's earnings] once and for all. He levied *itawa* [protection money] only on the notables and well-to-do in order to spend it on the poor and disabled. He conquered the *futuwwas* of neighbouring *haras,* thereby bringing to our *hara* a respect it had never enjoyed before that it came to be highly regarded beyond its area as much as it enjoyed internally justice, dignity and security.'[171] If we translate mythical language into political language rendering government for *fatwana*, exploitative capitalism for *baltaga*, taxation for *itawa,* nation for *hara* and neighbouring nations for the other *haras*, then we will have a pretty good, if somewhat simplistic, view of Mahfouz's conditions for the achievement of social harmony as well as harmony among nations.

At 60 but unruffled by his years, still loved and feared and in total control of a happy *hara*, Ashur unaccountably disappears. One day he simply does not return from his habitual nocturnal vigil outside the *takiyya.* Already adored by the *harafish* as a hero and a saint, his mysterious disappearance propels him on to an even higher plane of sanctity. After the initial shock, the frantic search and desperate wait, hope of Ashur's return is given up and a physical contest for the *fatwana* over the *hara* is won by his youthful son, Shams al-Din, whose reign, despite the temptations he is subjected to, continues along the just rules laid by his father. On Shams al-Din's death his son Sulayman takes over unchallenged. For a few years he follows in the footsteps of his father and grandfather, leading a poor and righteous life and putting *fatwana* in the service of the people. Then his eye is caught by the beauty of a wealthy man's daughter. The notables of the *hara* see it as their chance. The girl is offered to him in marriage. Although Sulayman offers no concessions at the beginning, a *de facto* alliance is sealed between the soldiery and the plutocracy of the *hara*. It is only a matter of time before Sulayman gives up his humble job as cart-driver and gives in to a luxurious lifestyle made possible by his wife's rich family. Gradually the interests of the *harafish* are neglected and Sulayman becomes the *futuwwa* of the rich. His link with the noble heritage of his forebears is severed and his children by his new wife grow up to be successful middle-class merchants. As he indulges in a life of leisure and pleasure, Sulayman gradually loses his health and fitness (essential assets for a *futuwwa*). He ends up a bedridden paralytic, the wreck of a one-time mighty man. One of his henchmen soon declares himself *futuwwa*. Thus the Nagis lose the *fatwana* for the first time in three generations and the *hara* enters into an age of darkness not unlike its 'pre-diluvian' days. The divine flame once lit by Ashur and maintained by Shams al-Din is extinguished.

The above events occupy three of the ten tales of the novel. The rest of the tales are variations on the same theme tracing the history of the al-Nagi family from one generation to another and the history of *fatwana* in the *hara*. *Fatwana* is no longer a monopoly of the Nagis, but it makes no difference any more to the *harafish* who is *futuwwa*, for now the descendants of the great Ashur can be as corrupt and tyrannical as any other *futuwwa*. Although the pattern of the book depends on repetition, there is enough variation to preclude tedium and a sense of suspense is maintained, unlike the case in *Children of the Alley* where suspense is pre-empted by the external framework of reference.

As we move from tale to tale and from generation to generation, Mahfouz succeeds in conveying a sense of the passage of time through sustained reference in highly poetic language, within and across tales, to the movement of time, the sequence of seasons, time's chariot, the ageing process, the rising and setting of the sun, the changes of climate, the changes of heart, the changes of fortune and the mutability of all things. All this exercises a cumulative if imperceptible effect on us, so that by the time we come to the end of the book we are left with the vague feeling that we have been reading the full story of time and man. The tragedy of humanity through the ages is emphasised by a sense of the immutability of place in the novel. Thus, although the novel spans some 16 generations on the realistic level (or man's time from Adam till now if we consider the symbolic level), the *hara* evinces little or no physical change throughout, nor do the power structure and relationship between rich and poor, strong and weak. If anything, this is an indictment of the human experience for its ethical failure despite all the material progress it may boast (this is probably why all signs of such progress are absent from the description of life in the *hara* in spite of the huge time span).

Time is of the essence in *Harafish*; it is not there only as the background against which the flux of human misery unfolds, but time itself, with its ultimate manifestation as death, is at the very core of the human tragedy. This of course is a favourite theme of Mahfouz's that predates *Harafish*. Nevertheless, one of his most haunting treatments of the subject remains that in the seventh tale of *Harafish*, entitled 'King Galal'. Galal is a late descendant of Ashur al-Nagi and one of the most powerful and evil *futuwwas* to have controlled the *hara*. His tragedy begins in his boyhood when he witnesses the head of his beautiful and adored mother smashed to pieces by a jealous ex-husband of hers. He never forgets the scene or learns to live with its consequences. He grows up with the agonising questions, 'Why do days not go back as they go forward? Why do we lose what we love and suffer what we hate? Why do things submit to irrevocable ordainments?'[172] One day he puts the question to his teacher at the *kuttab* (Koran school), 'Why do we die?' he asks. 'It is God's wisdom', replies the Shaykh. 'But *why?*' insists Galal. And this time he gets a flogging for an answer.[173]

As he advances in his teens he falls in love with Qamar, the daughter of a rich branch of the family. The girl reciprocates his love but the family stands in the way. In the end, however, they succumb to the will of the lovers. The girl becomes the centre of Galal's existence and for once he seems on the point of reaching reconciliation with life. Then in the midst of their preparations for the wedding, Qamar is taken ill. Within days 'things submit again to the irrevocable ordainments': death snatches Galal's bride. With her Galal's soul dies its final death, though he continues to live for many years. In his forlorn state he comes to define death as 'the only truth' and also as the only enemy. He condemns people because 'they sanctified death and worshipped it, thereby encouraging it until it turned into an immortal truth'.[174] Sitting in front of the *takiyya* one night he wonders what Qamar looked like in her grave: 'A swollen waterskin giving off foul smell floating in toxic liquids where worms dance. Do not mourn her who was quick to acknowledge defeat! She who did not keep her promise. She who showed no respect for love. She who did not cling to life and opened her chest unto death. We live or die by the strength of our will. There is nothing more revolting than victims! Advocates of defeat! Those who cheer that death is the end of everything living. That it is the ultimate truth. They make death with their weakness and their illusions. We are immortal and only die through treachery and weakness.'[175]

Armed with this vision and his Herculean build, Galal does not find it difficult to conquer the existing *futuwwa* and restore *fatwana* to the Nagi family. Soon his power extends unchallenged over his own *hara* and all the neighbouring ones. For a while the hopes of the *harafish* stir, as do the fears of the well-to-do. But nothing is further from Galal's mind than the suffering of the *hara*. His thoughts are focused on the ancestral grave awaiting him, notwithstanding the glory and the wealth and the indomitable strength. Overwhelmed with his existential despair, he allows the social cause to recede into insignificance. When told that people are wondering when he will set about restoring justice to the *hara*, he dismisses the matter scornfully: 'Why don't they give in to hunger as they give in to death?' he asks.[176] Despite his naturally ascetic temperament, he indulges in the accumulation of wealth and all things worldly 'as if he were barricading himself against death'.[177] And all the time he is haunted by the images of his mother's smashed head and his bride's lifeless face. In his obsessive search for a means of fighting death, he obtains an expensive recipe from the herbalist of the *hara* which, in conjunction with moderation in food, drink and sex, should help him prolong his youth and strength. But this is not good enough for him: immortality is his quest. That, he is told, is an aspiration that no believer should entertain as it incurs eternal damnation and is only possible through 'twinning with the devil'.[178] For Galal nothing is more damnable than death. Like Faustus in German legend, he accepts the price of mutiny against the human lot. The price of the medium who would effect the twinning process includes Galal's largest apartment block, the construction in the *hara* of a grotesque red minaret, ten storeys high and without a mosque, and as an additional condition total isolation for a year, on the last day of which the twinning was to take effect, heralding life without end. Galal accepts and endures heroically his solitary confinement for a whole year. On the last day, as the appointed moment approaches, he 'stands naked in front of an open window and welcomes the sunshine washed in the wetness of winter ... He feels drunk with a new spirit filling his breast ... He has conquered time, having confronted it face to face for so long and without a companion. He shall not fear it any more. Let it threaten others with its ill-fated passage! He shall know no wrinkles, no greying of the hair and no weakening of the bones. His soul shall not betray him. Nor shall he be borne in a coffin or laid in a grave. This solid body shall not decompose. It shall not turn into dust. And he shall not taste of the sorrow of departing.'[179]

Galal rejoins the world and establishes himself anew as the supreme master of the *hara* and an invincible force beyond its borders. One night he pays a secret visit to the monstrous red minaret, standing in the midst of a wasteland and towering above everything in the *hara*: 'He climbed its staircase step by step until he reached the top balcony. He defied the biting cold of winter to which the whole universe had surrendered. He raised his head to the plethora of stars keeping vigil above him. Thousands of eyes twinkled high above, while everything below was sunk in the darkness. It might be that he did not climb but that he grew in stature as he should. He must always rise and rise. Purity was only possible through rising. At the pinnacle he would hearken to the speech of the planets, the whispers of space and the cravings of power and eternity, away from the plaintive moans and foul odours. At this minute the *takiyya* sang its songs of everlasting life; Truth unveiled scores of its hidden faces; and the Unknown laid bare its store of fates. From this balcony he would review the passing trail of generations and prepare a role for each one. Here he could join once and for all the family of heavenly bodies.'[180] In his description of Galal's thoughts in this and the preceding passage, and indeed throughout this amazing tale, Mahfouz dramatises mankind's most haunting dreams over the centuries, of power, continued life and the solution of the mysteries of existence. In his contempt for the weak and indifference to their suffering, he smacks of Nietzsche's superman who rises above good and evil. He also echoes the great dictators of history in their contempt for human life and pain. His ambition is lofty and admirable but his means are selfish and cruel. Mahfouz therefore reserves a horrid end for him to show that he is far from being his ideal of the evolutionary goal of mankind. Nevertheless, he is portrayed as a full tragic hero who commands our sympathy and respect for his stand against time and death and his readiness to pay the price for defying such fearful opponents.

Armoured with his illusion of eternal life, Galal drops all his previous moderation and inhibitions. He begins to eat and drink and smoke and fornicate excessively. His lust for life stops at no boundary. Zinat, his erstwhile one and only mistress, who loved him madly and had dreamt of bringing him round to marrying her, watches his transformation and the ebbing away of his fondness for her with growing jealousy and uncomprehending despair. Eventually she poisons him. He dies a painful death, incredulous until the end that his powerful foe had triumphed over him notwithstanding. Maddened by the fire in his stomach, he staggers out of the house into the dark sleeping *hara*. He stumbles into the donkey-trough and tries to extinguish the internal blaze by drinking from it. Later under torchlight the gigantic body of what was once the mighty and proud Galal was found in a heap at the trough, covered in hay and dung. There was eternity for the beholder! As always, death had the last laugh.

Since the now myth-enshrouded days of Ashur al-Nagi and his son Shams al-Din, the downtrodden *harafish* have seen no justice and known no happiness. Was there no way then out of this terrible condition that the *hara* had endured for so long? The answer to this question occurs in 'The Mulberry and the Bludgeon', the tenth and final tale of *Harafish*. The *hara* is living through one of its usual dark ages, and in a poor, one-parent family descended from the great Ashur al-Nagi, the youngest of three sons is called Ashur too (not in vain as we shall see). From an early age he works as a shepherd. He grows up to be a strong man, though his pleasant manner tended to hide his strength from the eyes of observers. From an early age he is also attracted to the *takiyya* with its mysterious and inspiring songs and to the stories of the exploits of his great ancestor and namesake. Ashur's eldest brother drifts away into a world of crime and unlawful wealth and when he is found out, he commits suicide. The ruling *futuwwa* banishes the whole family from the *hara* as a punishment for crimes they did not commit. Soon the second brother drifts away too. Thus only Ashur and his mother remain together. Exiled and homeless, Ashur decides to live with his mother in the cemetery until the conditions are right to go back.

In his exile he has ample time to contemplate his predicament and that of the *hara*. He comes to the conclusion that the worst weaknesses of mankind are their love of money power'. He also thinks hard about why the golden age created by his great ancestor suffered a setback after his death and has never been restored. Through his long meditations in the *khala'*, his nocturnal vigils by the *takiyya* and a visit in his sleep from his spiritual mentor, he formulates a vision of the answer and the way, which he sets about putting into action. Ashur al-Nagi, his grandfather, was a strong man with a vision and a great heart, who gave justice to the *harafish* as a free gift, which only depended on the goodwill of the giver. That was why justice did not survive its founder. Ashur II (as we might call him) was therefore to approach matters differently. The *harafish* must earn justice for themselves. He could help by providing initiative and strong leadership, but he would not fight their battle for them while they sat back and watched. Thus he begins to proselytise among them and prepare them for the day of confrontation. He teaches them that they should trust nobody, not even him, but only themselves. And he tells them of a strange dream in which he 'saw them carrying bludgeons' (the traditional weapon of *futuwwas* and their men).[181] At the right moment, Ashur II ends his exile and leads the *harafish* into battle. Their numerical superiority under the inspiring leadership of Ashur II soon brings them victory over their once fearful oppressors. Established as unrivalled *futuwwa* of the *hara*, Ashur II does not, however, lose sight of his prime objective: that of making the *harafish* masters of their destiny, and protecting them against setbacks. Thus he ordains that they should train their children in the arts of *fatwana*, 'so that no rascal or adventurer should one day find it possible to dominate them'.

Popular revolution then is the answer to oppression offered by Mahfouz. This is perfectly understandable, seen in the context of his glorification of Egypt's only popular revolution in its contemporary history (the 1919 revolution) and, conversely, his bitter disillusionment with the later military-led, superimposed coup/revolution of 1952. Uncharacteristically in the work of Mahfouz, *Harafish* has a happy, positive ending, as we have seen. It embodies what was hinted at, at the end of *Children of the Alley.* There we were left with the vague impression that some day Hanash would return with the magical science book and the runaway youths of the *hara* to restore Gabalawi's estate to its legitimate owners. In *Harafish* this is exactly what Ashur II does. There is no mention of science in *Harafish*, true. But then is not the organisation of society on sound, just and workable principles, as Ashur II does, the manifestation of a scientific spirit? Both *Children of the Alley* and *Harafish* would seem thus to uphold the ideal of popular revolution.

Points of comparison and contrast with *Children of the Alley* constantly emerge from a discussion of *Harafish.* Nor should we end this section without reference to another such point, which concerns the character of Ashur II whom the discerning reader will recognise to be inspired by the historical figure of the Prophet

Muhammad. Like him, he starts his working life as a shepherd. Muhammad was an orphan; Ashur loses his father at the age of six.[182] Muhammad was brought up by a wet-nurse called Halima al-Sa'diyya; Ashur's mother is given the name Halima al-Baraka. Ashur is described as enamoured of the *takiyya*, the *khala'* and the beauty of women,[183] and as combining a strong build and a good temperament,[184] all of which are attributes that would fit the Prophet too. In addition, Ashur's exile period in the cemetery followed by his victorious return to the *hara* and his demolition of the obscene red minaret built by Galal, would easily parallel Muhammad's forced *hijra* (or Flight) to Medina and later triumphant return to Mecca and his destruction of the idols at the Ka'ba. All this is on the level of factual detail; the thematic similarities between the objectives and achievements of the two characters are too obvious to need comment. Ashur II, then, is Mahfouz's second attempt at portraying the Prophet of Islam in fiction. (His first of course was the character of Qasim in *Children of the Alley*.) Artistically, the basic difference between the two portrayals is that Ashur's has a life of its own and fits snugly in the larger structure of the book, whereas Qasim's character draws what artificial life it possesses from its historical model. It is a mark of the extent of Mahfouz's artistic achievement in the second portrayal that the religious conservatives and fundamentalists who had protested so strongly (to the point of attempting to murder the author in 1994) at the representation of Muhammad and other sacred figures in *Children of the Alley* did not so much as mention *Harafish* in this connection: so subtle and independent of its historical model is the portrayal that it completely escaped the notice of those non-literary eyes.

No discussion of *Harafish* would be complete without special attention to the *takiyya* – a prominent motif in the novel and a great Mahfouzian symbol in this as in other works. The *takiyya*, as we have seen, made its first major appearance in the novelist's work in *Fountain and Tomb,* a work which pre-dated *Harafish* by only two years. It retains here the same symbolic value as it had there, as an embodiment of man's age-old yearning for Heaven, the hereafter, the supernatural, the metaphysical, the timeless, the infinite, the spiritual, the ideal, the absolute – or God, for the lack of a better and all-encompassing word. A focal point for the spiritual aspirations of the *hara*-dwellers, as well as the source of inspiration for Ashur al-Nagi and Ashur II, it must be remembered that it was also there, at the *takiyya*, that Galal received the revelatory impulse that led him on his destructive quest for power and eternity. This would appear to mean that the *takiyya* is what man makes of it. It is only the embodiment of a mystical yearning – it has no existence outside the soul of man. This interpretation is strengthened by the fact that nobody ever succeeds in establishing any form of communication with the *takiyya* and its dervish inhabitants. The gates are always closed and no one is ever let in or out. Even the most catastrophic events, like plagues and famines, seem to pass unnoticed by the *takiyya* in its eternal indifference to the *hara*. In the words of Shams al-Din, frustrated at the impervious silence of the *takiyya*: 'it is a witness who gives no testimony'.[185] Another alienating factor about the *takiyya* is the songs sung by the dervishes and overheard by outsiders. They are captivating and comforting but they are sung in a foreign language, incomprehensible to the *hara*, adding yet more to the general sense of mystery and inapproachability besetting the *takiyya.* Mahfouz has done well for his purpose to quote those Persian Sufi verses and scatter them all over the narrative, leaving them in their original tongue, as baffling to the Arab reader as they are to the people of the *hara* in the book. If the *takiyya* is a symbol of man's highest ideals, then the *qabw* or vault is one for his lowest instincts. Like the *takiyya*, it is a recurrent motif in the novel, always described as dark and filthy, a place for crime and illicit sex, and the abode of jinn and devils. Another motif of evil which joins the *qabw*, two-thirds through the book, is the red minaret without a mosque, built by Galal in his mad search for eternity. It survives his ignominious death for a long time: a token, in its crude phallic pride, of man's vanity and ultimate folly.

On the day of the demolition of this evil monstrosity at the behest of Ashur II, the *hara* celebrates boisterously well into the night. After midnight, Ashur II makes his way to the open space in front of the *takiyya* for some solitude within earshot of the songs. Then the impossible comes to pass: 'He squatted on the ground, giving in to a sense of contentment and a gentle breeze. It was one of those rare moments when life shed its veil to reveal the purity of its radiance. Nothing to complain of in body or soul, time or space. It was as if the mysterious songs were giving away their secrets in a thousand tongues – as if he now understood why for so long they had sung in an exotic tongue and kept their doors closed. Through the darkness wafted a creaking sound. Stunned, he gazed at the enormous gate. He saw it open smoothly and steadily. Out of it approached the shadowy figure of a dervish – an embodiment of night's breath. He leaned towards him. "Get ready with your pipes and drums!" he said. "Tomorrow the Grand Shaykh will leave his cloister and march through the *hara* in a halo of light. A bludgeon and a mulberry will he give unto each man. Get ready with your pipes and drums!"'[186]

This of course is only an inner vision (Mahfouz uses the word *ru'ya* (vision) to refer to the experience in the last paragraph of the novel). This is as it should be, since all communications between the *takiyya* and those attracted to it have been by means of inner vision or revelation. Nevertheless, it is a unique vision, not hitherto experienced by any of the most faithful devotees of the *takiyya*, not even the great Ashur al-Nagi himself. For the first time in its 'history', the *takiyya* opened its haughty, silent doors to a mortal of the *hara* and deigned to speak to him. What was more, a 'walkabout' by the Grand Shaykh himself was promised. This is nothing short of a meeting of the eternal and the temporal. This is the way to eternity. This is the path which Galal in his selfishness had been blinded to. Only a humanity that has achieved a total and lasting justice can aspire to eternity, can merge into a timeless union with the *takiyya*. Only then would the Grand Shaykh of the *takiyya* (or Gabalawi of the Great House) come out and give each man a mulberry (his share of the estate) and a bludgeon with which to defend it for ever. Only then would God descend to Earth, or Man climb to Heaven, for these are but paradoxically antonymous words with identical denotations.

Within five years of *Harafish*, Mahfouz published another episodic novel: *Arabian Nights and Days* (1982), in which he proceeded, as the title suggests, to appropriate and make his own no lesser a work than *The Thousand and One Nights.* Though he still had to write a handful of novels, it is *Arabian Nights and Days* that will no doubt be remembered as his last major work. Together with *Harafish*, it represents the peak of his episodic period. Rather than create his own myth to portray his vision of the human condition as he did in *Harafish*, here he chooses to adapt for the same purpose one of the most imaginative products of the human mind. The author chooses some 13 unconnected tales from *The Arabian Nights* (itself a work in episodic form) and renders them afresh through the techniques of modernism (symbolism, recurrent motifs, stream of consciousness and magical realism which comes naturally to an *Arabian Nights* context). Tales originally independent of each other are so manipulated that they join up in a narrative continuum. Characters continue to operate across tales and meet up with other characters, unlike in the original, while completely new characters and events are invented and incorporated in the book to serve the novelist's goals. All these technical, unity-forging factors are further strengthened by the work's thematic cohesion, as another Mahfouzian probing of the problems of social evil, time, and the human relationship with the absolute. The most unifying technique he uses, however, is one that he did not have to invent: the frame-story of Shahrazad and Shahrayar which holds the whole of *The Arabian Nights* together.

The novel begins where *The Arabian Nights* stopped. In other words, it is an attempt at portraying the conditions of Shahrayar, Shahrazad and their subjects after the end of the original frame story, i.e. after Shahrazad had finished telling her last story, given birth to the king's children and earned his pardon. The massacre of the virgins has now been over for some time and Shahrayar's lust for blood has abated and given place to a pensive mood. He is still, however, an unhappy man and his kingdom is a haven for injustice and corruption. Shahrazad is equally unhappy. Her marriage to him had been an act of self-sacrifice to stop the flow of blood, but she does not love him. Mahfouz indeed draws Shahrayar's character with great care, showing in a gradual and convincing fashion his development from a bloodthirsty tyrant to a just ruler and finally a bewildered man who renounces power and sets out on a journey in search of the meaning of existence, leaving behind a Shahrazad who has now begun to love him.

His wanderings lead him to the Weeper's Rock by the river. The rock opens to him. He enters and the door shuts behind him. He is overwhelmed by the beauty of the place, which 'was bright without a light, cool without a window and redolent with the scent of roses without a garden'.[187] The description goes on deeper and deeper into the realm of fantasy until it becomes clear that Shahrayar has stepped into Heaven itself where there is only joy and timelessness. But alas! Shahrayar stumbles into a little golden door with a warning on it saying, 'Entry forbidden' – the one and only prohibition in that blissful eternity. One day Shahrayar's resolve weakens. He opens the door only to find himself back on earth. Thus the cycle of sin (motivated by the desire to know) and punishment is completed. But we must note here a meaningful omission from the Biblical account: there is no snake, no evil and no woman. Shahrayar's fall is of his own making: responsibility for man's choices rests with no other party than himself, Mahfouz would have us believe. Shahrayar returns to earth, but his soul remains attached to Heaven – to the ideal world that he has seen with his mind's eye.

Published one year after *Arabian Nights and Days*, *The Journey of Ibn Fattouma* (1983) constitutes Mahfouz's last panoramic review of human history. Although a short novel, the broadness of its scope puts it on a footing with works like *Children of the Alley* and *Harafish*. Like them, it is episodic in form with the episodes representing progress in time. Time here, however, is not only that of the novel's action, but rather mankind's time from the dawn of organised society to the present day. For the 'journey' of the novel is on the allegorical level, made through time rather than space. In essence, the book is nothing but a conducted tour in social and political history. The novel evokes the atmosphere and format of medieval Arabic *rihla* or travel literature, particularly the journeys of Ibn Battuta, the illustrious 14th-century Arab traveller, as recorded in his famous book *Rihlat Ibn Battuta*, of which Mahfouz's novel is by and large a parody. The novel covers six journeys to six countries with fictitious names, though we can tell from the context what they stand for. There is no specific reference to time either, though the context and the means of travel etc suggest that it is medieval times. Thus it appears that time and place are intentionally defaced. This, as we have seen, is an artistic technique previously used by the author to underline the universality of his themes – that of *The Journey of Ibn Fattouma* being the search for the ideal human society and the political/economic system capable of achieving it.

Ibn Battuta's original motive when he left Tangier in 1326 at the age of 21 was to perform the religious duty of the *hajj* (the pilgrimage to Makka).[188] In the event he went round most of the known world of his day and returned some 25 years later. His fictitious descendant, however, knew his own mind better and had his journey planned out in the minutest detail before he set out. Nothing, though, was further from his mind than *hajj*. He is a man of an inquisitive mind, a perturbed soul and a socio-political awareness. Though himself well-to-do by inheritance, he is dissatisfied with his homeland *Dar al-Islam* (The Abode of Islam) because it is full of injustice, poverty and ignorance, and because there 'every action whether beautiful or ugly is initiated in the name of God the Compassionate, the Merciful.'[189] He thus curses *Dar al-Islam* as an 'abode of falsity,'[190] and is determined to travel in order 'to learn and bring back to my sick country the healing remedy'.[191] (This is central to the parody since Ibn Battuta, by contrast, idealises *Dar al-Islam* in his own *rihla*.[192]) Having a more ambitious goal for his *rihla* than his historic progenitor, Ibn Fattouma meets with less success. He never returns to his homeland and the novel ends with the search as yet unfinished. Within the allegorical framework of the book this ending is perhaps the only conceivable one: humanity's quest for social utopia is an ongoing endeavour.

'Have a good journey,' my friend and teacher said as he bade me farewell. 'God willing, you will come upon that which you seek.' I was delighted as radiant thoughts rained down upon me, reflecting their loveliness upon my soul, and the hearts of the beneficent beat with sympathy. I did not want for food, drink, or clothing – nor forgot my city the whole time I was gone. When I finally returned, my friend and teacher asked me, 'Did you find what you were looking for?' 'I will find it here,' I replied, 'amongst the agonies, as well as the hopes – via my vision as an explorer, and my patience as one who abides in one place.'

'Dream 181' from *Dreams of Departure*

The publication in 1987 of *Morning and Evening Talk* brings Mahfouz's episodic phase to an end. In fact, and with the benefit of hindsight, it was to be his penultimate novel. Here he uses again the technique of alphabetically arranged character sketches first used some 15 years earlier in *Mirrors*. It contains 67 character sketches drawn mainly from three families whose members are all related either through blood or intermarriage. Though of moderate length, it is Mahfouz's most ambitious *roman fleuve*, tracing the lives of three whole families across five generations and a period of nearly 200 years. Thus *Morning and Evening Talk* has its beginning in the late 18th century, namely with the arrival of Napoleon in Egypt, and concludes with occurrences from the post-Sadat era, which makes it an account of the evolution of Egypt from medievalism to modernity, though the grip of the past is shown to have remained firm throughout.

Morning and Evening Talk is a sad novel. On the public level, it amounts to an elegy to the failure of the experiment of modernisation in Egypt. On the private level, it is a bizarre celebration of death, of the incessant massacre by time of men's hopes and lives. Each of the 67 sketches contains in a very condensed manner a whole lifetime, always beginning with birth and almost always ending with death. Considering the lexicographical arrangement of the sketches, we are made to feel that individuals are no more than short, insignificant entries in the huge, ongoing lexicon of time.

The Little Pieces of Clay: The Novelist as Short Story Writer and Dramatist

If Mahfouz had not written any of his novels, he would still have merited a place of high prominence in the history of modern Arabic literature on account of his short stories alone, of which he published well over 250 spread across no less than 16 collections and a lifetime. As it happens he has also written, as we have seen, 33 novels, the inevitable result of which has been that his short stories have mostly been accorded second place in the study of the author's work and treated all too often as footnotes to the novels, this book regrettably being no exception. One critic has described the relationship of the short stories to the novels in terms of 'the little pieces of clay left over after the manufacture of earthenware … the remainder of characters, events and thoughts from his long works'.[193] This statement should not be taken as dismissive of the short stories; it only seeks to point out that both the stories and novels draw from the same intellectual substance. But as works of art to be read and enjoyed, and as edifiers of the human soul, their independence and importance in their own right can only be self-evident.

The early and mid-career collections
Mahfouz started writing stories while he was still an undergraduate. His first known published story goes back to 1932. Regular publication, however, did not begin until after his graduation in 1934.

By 1946 he had published 74 stories altogether in the various literary and general magazines of the day in Cairo.[194] At a date that has so far been difficult to determine with precision (but which we know must be at least later than April 1945) he collected 28 of these stories (presumably, the ones he considered to be the best) and published them under the title *Whispers of Madness*,[195] with some of the ones he neglected selected and published as late as 2001 by novelist Muhammad Jibril under the title *Futuwwat al-'Utuf* (The 'Utuf Thug'). Today these stories, very like the early historical novels, are only of 'historical' value, as the primitive stages in the evolution of a prodigious talent. They are written in a prose style as yet unliberated from classical ornateness and cliché, and influenced by Egypt's great sentimentalist of the day, Mustafa Lutfi al-Manfaluti (1876–1924). Structurally, they are weak, tending to rely heavily on coincidence and improbable situations, while the author is ever intrusively present with cumbersome didactic comment. Nevertheless, for all their faults and artistic immaturity, one can see (in their preoccupations at least) that these stories were written by the Mahfouz-to-be. The roots of the author's socialism and nationalism are there, as are those of his life-long obsession with time and the ironies of fate, however simple and less than half-formed. There, too, are the blueprints for some of his typical characters and situations. Finally, there too are the roots of the author's tragic sense of life and his profound sadness for the individual, twice crushed by the injustice of society and the less tractable harshness that is at the centre of existence.

By the time Mahfouz came to collect and publish the stories of *Whispers of Madness*, he had already published his first six novels and made the shift from historical romance to realism. For the next 15 years or so it would appear that the short story was but a fleeting passion of early youth or the training ground for the author's real mission. Those years were spent in perfecting the techniques of realism up to *The Trilogy* and the allegorical *Children of the Alley.* They also saw the increasing use of the stream-of-con-sciousness technique and the final shift from traditional, omnis-cient narration to the restricted viewpoint; from the sprawling novel to the condensed plot and the poetic, taut and symbol-strewn prose style. During that period, too, the author's meta-physical quest for God and the meaning of existence had begun to dominate his work. In 1963, however, much to the surprise of his critics, Mahfouz (now a mature, established novelist) published a second collection of short stories, *God's World*,[196] on which all the above accomplishments were brought to bear. Moreover, the following years were soon to prove that this newly rediscovered passion was there to stay and effloresce, mostly in line with his novelistic development, but sometimes taking wild turns of its own and unleashing in the author fresh powers of creativity untapped in the novels (as happened in the post-1967 Absurd explosion). By a strange irony, Mahfouz who started his writing career with short stories, ended it also with short stories. His last novel was published almost 18 years before his death, during which period he only expressed himself through the medium of the short story and other even shorter genres such as the aphoristic narrative or parable as we shall see in the next chapter. To friends and interviewers he blamed it on old age and declining health which precluded the effort writing a novel demanded.[197]

God's World is predominantly an awed and bewildered con-templation of the mysterious phenomenon of death: seven of its 14 stories deal with the subject through haunting metaphors and situations. The subject of 'God', being likewise an aspect of the metaphysical, is never too far from that of 'death'; it is no wonder that in the proximity of so much death in *God's World,* we encounter 'Zaabalawi',[198] the author's most celebrated metaphor for a sick humanity's persistent search for an ever-elusive God, a search which is at once its pain and its hope.[199]

In 1965 the collection *A House of Ill Repute* was published to show Mahfouz still haunted by visions of death and trying to purge his awe in one metaphor after another: 11 out of the 18 stories of the collection are treatments of the fearful subject. Interestingly, the stories in the collection generally display in their artistic conception and execution a strong affinity with his contemporaneous novels. They too are metaphors well grounded in realistic detail, while pointing at a higher symbolic meaning.

War and the Absurd

In 1969 Mahfouz published two collections: *The Black Cat Tavern* and *Under the Bus Shelter.* The first of these two collections comprises 19 stories, which mostly share with the two previous ones their thematic and stylistic features, with God, death, time and above all the ironies of fate dominating the stories. Though published in 1969, it appears, however, that most of the stories in this collection were written prior to the national trauma of 1967, since none of them (with the possible exception of the title-story) demonstrates the tremendous effect that the events of 1967 were to have for a while on Mahfouz's work. This effect is in fact to be found, to start with, in the second collection of the same year, *Under the Bus Shelter.* Indeed, the author goes out of his way to ensure that his readers are aware of the specific historical context against which the stories were written: on the back of the flyleaf he records uncharacteristically that *these stories were written in the period between October and December 1967.* That is to say, they were his first reaction in art form to the national catastrophe of 5 June 1967. The collection contains six stories and five one-act plays, all of which with the exception of two represent a substantial departure from the author's habitual way of recreating external reality in his work up to that time. What we experience here is an expressionist or even surrealist reality characterised by a total collapse of rationality and structure. The world these works present us with is one where conclusions bear no relevance to premises and where language is no guarantee of communication. It is also a world without a sense of purpose, a world where anarchy, futility and violence reign supreme. In short, it is a world depicted in the best traditions of the literature of the absurd. The fatal passivity of a society of indifferent onlookers is recreated in 'Taht al-mazalla' (Under the Bus Shelter), where a group of people waiting for the bus (which never arrives) watch, taking place under their noses, thefts, murders, deadly car crashes, burial of the living, sex orgies, decapitated heads rolling at their feet – all without lifting a finger. When finally they approach a policeman, who has been happily looking on all the time, he charges them with illegal assembly and guns them down on the spot.

Mahfouz's sudden headlong dive into surrealist and absurdist modes of expression left critics reeling from the impact of the surprise. True, he had earlier given expression to issues of an absurdist, existentialist nature (such as in *The Beggar* and *Adrift on the Nile*), but this was mainly done through a rationalist mode of narrative which showed a certain respect for external reality. This was now no longer the case, with the artistic reality badly distorted to reflect the disintegration of the society on which it sought to comment. The author was showered with questions from astounded critics and curious interviewers. Always happy to comment on his work, he provided the answers. In his pronouncements on the subject he appears well aware that his version of *absurdity* is one that is highly structured and fraught with *meaning*. He refers, almost apologetically, to the period in which he wrote the stories as one during which he *had lost his balance* and thus came *to write works which were seemingly absurd*. He goes on to say: *However, my insistence on* [social] *commitment spoiled their absurdity ... In those works I painted a world that was confused, fragmented and devoid of logic or reason. But it was apparent, despite this, that there was a certain meaning that I was driving at ... It appears that I had not completely given in to the absurd.*[200] Mahfouz's affair with the absurd was to prove a passing, if intense, infatuation and was not to spill over from his stories and playlets into his novels. By the early 1970s the whole episode was over and for a long time after, the author was at pains to distance himself from it. *I do not believe in the philosophy of the absurd ... Absurdity believes in nothing, whereas I have many things that I believe in. Absurdity finds no meaning in life, whereas to me it is full of meaning. Absurdity, in its grief before death, is oblivious of civilisation, whereas before civilisation I tend to ignore death.*[201]

The plays and the dialogue-based stories

Mahfouz's absurdist phase coincided with another no less astounding development in his creative life. Nearly 60 years of age with some 30 years of writing behind him, during which he had established himself as the unrivalled novelist of Arabic, he started to publish in *al-Ahram* a series of one-act plays which he collected later in *Under the Bus Shelter*, as mentioned above. The plays, if anything, are even more steeped in absurdity than the contemporary stories. But, as in the stories again, it is Mahfouz's own brand of 'meaningful absurdity'. All five plays appear to be concerned with examining certain negative and positive values, which by their presence in or absence from Egyptian life led, in the author's view, to the 1967 debacle. This is achieved from behind a screen of abstraction and distortion. No particularly Egyptian scene is evoked, nor is the 1967 defeat mentioned. The characters are nameless, while the stage settings are mostly frugal and expressionistic in nature. The dialogue, which is written in simple standard Arabic, is often witty and racy, maintaining a quick rhythm through generally short speeches and occasional repartee. 'Yumit wa yuhyi' (Death and Resurrection) examines the trepidations of a young man faced with a menacing danger and torn between his love for life and sense of dignity. In the end the play appears to laud freedom as an absolute value that should be maintained even in the face of death. 'Al-Tirka' (The

Legacy) examines the debilitating tensions between the spiritual 'legacy' of the past and the necessity of scientific progress at the expense of this legacy. The ironically titled 'al-Najat' (Rescue), on the other hand, dramatises the fear, the despondency, the sense of siege and finally the gratuitous death of the individual living under a police state. 'Mashru˓ lil-munaqasha' (A Project for Debate) portrays a dogmatic tyrannical playwright, who refuses to consider the views of his actors and director of a play he is writing. In 'al-Mahamma' (The Task), the fifth and last play in this collection, fantasy and abstraction are again placed in the service of a sharp intellectual message, which consists in the disparagement of passivity and inaction.

Mahfouz's flirtation with the theatre, which appeared to be an integral part of his short-lived connection with the absurd, came to an end more or less at the same time as the latter did. He explained his shift to drama in the aftermath of 1967 in an interview given in 1970: *There is no doubt that today we live in the age of the theatre. The present moment* [in our history]*, fraught with ideas and problems, can only be debated through the theatre … The novel needs calmness, consideration and settled conditions, and because of this it must now step aside and let the theatre take control.*[202] In addition to the five one-act plays included in *Under the Bus Shelter* referred to above, Mahfouz included three more in later collections (which brings his total output for the theatre to eight plays).

In 1971, he published two further collections of short stories: *A Tale without Beginning or End* and *The Honeymoon.* Some of the stories were now written in Mahfouz's old familiar style of symbolic or two-layered realism, but the majority were still characterised by a wild imagination scornful of observable reality. The themes all came from his customary repertoire with its persistent preoccupation with Egypt's immediate political and cultural crises. The stories are at times limited to portraying social disaffection, and at others go on to point to the author's vision of a way out, which consists invariably in commitment to responsibility, facing up to reality and the adoption of a scientific outlook. Strikingly, most of the stories in both collections are dominated by dialogue, with narrative interspersions often needing nothing much more than brackets to turn them into stage directions. Conscious of their peculiar quality, the author coined the word *huwariyya* (a dialogic story) to describe this particular type of story.[203]

Back to reality

The barrage of short stories which took the shape of four collections published between 1969 and 1971 was temporarily interrupted to herald the author's return to novel writing with *Mirrors* in 1972 and *Love in the Rain* in 1973. The first novel's episodic form and the second's lack of a central plot or character, however, show the author to have been still in a mood which inclined to, as it were, the piecemeal rather than the wholesale contemplation of reality. In 1973 another collection of stories was published under the title *The Crime.* The collection is largely a continuation of the expressionist-cum-surrealist trend discussed above. Thematically, the stories point at a relaxation in the persistent preoccupation with the immediate political reality which characterised the earlier collections. Most of the stories here are forays into the author's usual metaphysical haunts. In retrospect, *The Crime* was largely to mark the end of the absurdist connection in Mahfouz's career.

After *The Crime* there was to be a lull in the publication of short stories for a period of about five years, during which Mahfouz produced five novels including his highly innovative work *Harafish.* In 1979, however, two further collections were published, namely *The Devil Preaches* and *Love under the Pyramids.* Both collections are dominated by longish stories averaging 40–50 pages. The staccato prose, often poetic, pensive and full of a sense of wonder at the nature of things, reveals a close affinity with the style of the contemporarily-published *Harafish.* In their socio-political scope, the stories are a testimony to Mahfouz's untiring, almost stoical, effort to keep up with the woes of his nation. This is a task which he undertook for over half a century and under a variety of regimes and social conditions, yet he always managed to sense with an unfailing instinct what was wrong with his country and be the first to give it expression: it is no wonder that he has often been described as the conscience of his nation. In these collections the pain and confusion of the post-1967 years is no longer there. Meanwhile another Arab-Israeli war had come and gone. The Suez Canal was crossed, the Bar-Lev Line destroyed, and the myth of the invincibility of Israel laid to rest. This, coupled with the measured political and economic liberalisation initiated by a buoyant and self-confident Sadat in the mid-1970s, helped boost the public morale for a while. But the Sadat promise proved a fiction all too soon with the euphoria of the military achievement of October 1973 giving way again to political stalemate; democratisation proving to be only surface-deep; and *infitah* or economic liberalisation creating a new class of the super-rich rather than bringing plenty to the many.

Mahfouz, whose nationalist and artistic instincts simply rejected the passing euphoria and showed no trace of it in his work, was quick to capture the new frustration and disaffection in his stories of the late 1970s. Official corruption, abuse of power, political manipulation of the justice system, illegitimate wealth, the displacement of the middle class in the consumerist society created by the *infitah* policy, unemployment, shortage of housing, the sexual frustration of a generation of young people crippled on the one hand by a conservative social attitude to premarital sex, and too economically constrained, on the other, to afford marriage – all these issues and, above all, the crack under their pressure in individual morality and the loss of belief in social ideals, are widely recreated by Mahfouz in many of the stories of *The Devil Preaches* and *Love under the Pyramids*.

But alert as he is to the crude and humdrum necessities of human life and never oblivious to their importance in determining individual action and shaping social movement, Mahfouz has remained at all times preoccupied to the point of obsession with the pursuit of a truth higher than anything that the physical world or history can offer us for the comprehension of ourselves – that kind of truth we normally call God. In these collections, as elsewhere in his work, physical hunger and spiritual thirst go hand in hand. Thus in proximity with the stories dealing with issues of society we find as many dealing with the holy quest or (as often in Mahfouz) inseparably combining the two pursuits. In 'al-Rajul al-thani' (The Second Man), to take an example from *The Devil Preaches*, the author explores the concept of man's God-appointed mission on earth through the intriguing metaphor of a *futuwwa* (strongman/thug) who elects one of his men to carry out a mysterious and impossible task, promising him the position of 'second man' in the gang if successful. As the situation grows more complex and one error leads to another, the *futuwwa* offers his man no guidance whatsoever, enigmatically ordering him at each turn to 'continue' with the task. Finally, the aspiring man dies in the pursuit of a mission whose meaning or goal he never comprehended. But until the end he refuses to contemplate the notion that perhaps his chief was playing a practical joke on him – that there was no mission and no goal; that it was all absurd.

In 1982 Mahfouz published a collection titled *I Saw in a Dream*, followed in 1984 by yet another, *The Secret Organisation*. The stories of these collections represent yet further variations on the author's familiar repertoire of themes, his inventive powers apparently never failing to find fresh and memorable metaphors for old concerns. The prose is often lyrical and evocative, while the narrative technique tends to depend on dreams, visions and the interweaving of the realistic and the fantastic; a style that Mahfouz was later in the 1990s to develop further into a new genre based on aphoristic or parabolic narratives and dreams.

The late collections

The next collection, entitled *The False Dawn*, came in 1989, containing no less than 30 very short stories averaging about five pages each. Most of the stories are of a social or political documentary nature, while a few continue with the metaphysical search. One deserving special mention is a four-page story, 'Nisf yawm' (Half a Day), which merges, in one moment of time, the consciousness of the protagonist both as a child passing his first day at school and as an old man unable to cross a busy road. It is a technical *tour de force* achieving verbally what even film may find difficult to achieve. Brief as it is, the story must count as the author's most powerful rendering of the dilemma of the gulf between observable time and mnemonic time.[204]

'Half a Day', nostalgic, hanging on to things past and taking refuge in memory from the onslaught of Time, sets the tone for the work to follow in the 1990s, as in the stories of Mahfouz's two last collections: *The Final Decision* (1996) and *Echo of Oblivion* (1999) (in Arabic *al-Qarar al-akhir* and *Sada al-nisyan* respectively). A story titled 'The Cradle' in *The Final Decision* and consisting in nothing but lyrical images of a happy childhood, recalled by a consciousness alienated in old age from changing times, opens with these wistful recollective words which set the tone of the whole collection; indeed the whole output of Mahfouz's last works: 'In the midst of afflictions, it will do no harm to seek refuge in the company of the things once cherished by the heart. Those too were real with roots struck deep in life. He who feels hot is entitled to dry his sweat and quench his thirst.'[205] Consistent with the contemplation of a life gone by is a preoccupation with death. A story titled 'Traveller with hand luggage only' depicts the thoughts of a dead man who does not realise he has died and thinks he is on a train journey. But when the train moves after the goodbyes, he 'realises for the first time that he is the only passenger in the whole carriage. How strange! For years the train has never left with a single seat unoccupied. What a strange day this has been! ... But there will be time to think about all that has happened and to try to understand ...'[206]

Mahfouz's obsession in old age with 'the things once cherished by the heart' is behind the stories of *Echo of Oblivion*, all set in the mythologised *haras* of the Jamaliyya of his childhood and thronged by its people, familiar from earlier fiction. His quest for the re-creation of the past is epitomised in a fascinating story by the title 'Ascension to the Moon', in which the narrator, a persona for Mahfouz, instructs an architect to rebuild on the empty spot where his childhood house once stood the exact same house again with the old design, dimensions and layout in stark contempt for the spirit of the times. When the job is completed, the narrator starts to climb the stairs of the house, and a flood of happy images and voices from his childhood engulfs him. As he reaches the roof, the evening '... was beginning to descend on the quarter from behind the domes and minarets of mosques. The moon ascended proudly from behind the old houses and I gazed on it adoringly, at which point I was raised high above shoulder level. "Take it if you can," whispered the kind voice. With infinite love and anticipation, I put out my arm to the radiant moon.'[207] The narrative blends into one the moment of remembrance and the moment remembered: mnemonic time triumphs over real time; not an unusual trick for the aged Mahfouz, as we have seen in the contemporary story of 'Half a Day'.

Remembrance of Things Past and Dreams of Death and the Hereafter

In his old age, Mahfouz's writing fell in the grip of a permanent sense of nostalgia, a pained hankering after times past, places ravaged by Time, Death (never far from his thoughts at any time) and people departed. As the world and people he knew fast disappeared, he increasingly took refuge in memory, which provided a semblance of permanence in the face of the inexorable mutability of all things around him. This resulted in a number of lyrical and highly personal works driven by a desire to recapture the past in prose. These works can be traced back to the mid-1970s with *Fountain and Tomb*, gradually escalating in frequency and intensity to become almost his only mode of expression from the 1990s and until his death in 2006.

His last novel, *Qushtumur Café*, as well as *Morning and Evening Talk*, and a collection of short stories titled *Good Morning to You*, published in rapid succession over a two-year period (1987–8), all bear the hallmarks of this last phase of Mahfouz's creative career. They are all set between Jamaliyya and Abbasiyya, the two parts of Cairo that witnessed his childhood and early youth, and all have a recollective, nostalgic tone in which the novelist's own voice can often be discerned, and characters and events appear to be largely drawn from his personal remembrance of the period. Together they are a homage to the past. The evocative opening paragraph of *Qushtumur Café* is a good example: 'Abbasiyya in its bygone youth:

an oasis in the heart of an expansive desert. In the east stood castle-like mansions and in the west small houses which took pride in their newness and their back gardens. Surrounded by vegetable fields, palm and henna trees and groves of prickly pears, it sank in a sweet tranquillity and an all-encompassing peacefulness, interrupted from time to time by the buzz of the white tram travelling endlessly along its route between Heliopolis and al-'Ataba al-Khadra. And from the desert a dry breeze would blow over it, borrowing from the fields on its way their scents, thereby stirring in the hearts their secretly cherished loves. *But* [my italics] in the evening a beggarly minstrel roams its streets, barefoot, goggle-eyed and wearing a threadbare galabiya. He plays his *rabab* [a simple, normally single-stringed instrument] and sings in a harsh but penetrating voice: "I put my trust in you, O Time, but you betrayed me."'[208]

The first sentence of the novel is a compression of its entire meaning. Abbasiyya was once a youthful *place* but *time* has passed and made sure that its youth is now a 'bygone' fact. Abbasiyya of course is not an abstract place but a quarter of Cairo inhabited by people and its 'bygone youth' is also theirs, and the whole novel is simply an act of resistance against time by the only human faculty capable of it: memory. The memory here is that of the narrator, largely a persona for Mahfouz, and the whole tragedy lies in '*But*' of the penultimate sentence above, that *but* which is latent in the passage (as in the nature of things) from the first moment. The fact that Abbasiyya's youth is introduced as 'bygone' implies that the description that follows of the quarter as a piece of eternity whose beauty knows no withering and tranquillity no disturbance is merely a trick of recollection, while the poor minstrel's lament over the fickleness of time sums up the human condition. There is nothing substantially new about Mahfouz's last novel. It does not amount to much more than a variation on *There Only Remains an Hour*. All its characters are borrowed with only cosmetic changes from previous works and so are the public and private events. There is nothing new either in its view of man and society or in the author's reading of his country's socio-political history in the 20th century. Its value lies in none of this, but in the gush of nostalgia which impelled Mahfouz to write it, in his memory's desperate grip on time and his poetic evocation of its fleeting images.

Inventive and experimental in form, style and content to the end, two works stand out in Mahfouz's last ten years: *Echoes of an Autobiography* (1996), and *The Dreams* (2004) and its sequel, *Dreams of Departure* (2007).[209] Just as he surprised his readers with the 'episodic novel' in the 1970s and 1980s, he was to surprise them again with another innovative, narrative form with the publication of *Echoes of an Autobiography*, first serialised in *al-Ahram* newspaper in February-April 1994 before appearing in book form in 1996. The book consists of a large number of very short self-contained sayings, covering a wide range of themes, often telling a story or describing a situation in lyrical evocative language imbued with Sufi or mystic profundity that calls to mind such works as Nietzsche's *Thus Spoke Zarathustra* (1883–85) and *The Prophet* (1923) by Gibran Khalil Gibran (1883–1931).

> *Literature that does not rise to the level of poetry – whether it takes the form of verse or prose – bears no relation to literature at all.*[210]
>
> Naguib Mahfouz

For the lack of a better term, I will call the new form the 'aphoristic or parabolic narrative'. Many of those aphoristic narratives were based on events in the author's life, which is why he calls his abstractions of them 'Echoes of an Autobiography', having at first considered calling them 'Meditations'.[211] Strictly speaking, there is nothing more remote from an 'autobiography' than these symbolic mini-narratives. Mahfouz's autobiography was never written and the closest we can get to one is in such fictional recreations of his life as in *The Trilogy* and *Fountain and Tomb*, works

Mahfouz watches the Nobel ceremony on television at home with his wife

which he has consistently admitted to be based on phases of his life. What we have in *Echoes of an Autobiography* is the quintessence of the wisdom of a lifetime.

One can talk of a number of axes around which the narratives revolve in no particular order. Those axes are the selfsame ones that were at the centre of his life's work: time, memory, death, fate, coincidence, God, reason, love, politics, Sufism and work as an absolute human value. In a way those pithy enchanting contemplations of life, full of a sense of wonder at the inscrutability of the world, present us with the epitome of Mahfouz's view of the human condition previously spread over thousands of pages. Dominant is a sense of nostalgia for the past with its people and places, and sorrow for the ephemeral nature of youth and joyful times, as in the following episode of 'Living Pictures': 'This old picture brings together the members of my family, and this other one is of friends from long ago. I looked at them both for so long that I sank into memories of the past. All the faces were cheerfully radiant and at ease, eloquent with life. There was no hint, not the slightest, of what lay hidden in the unknown. And they had all passed on, not a single one remained. Who can determine that life was a living reality and not a dream or an illusion?'[212]

Stronger than Forgetfulness

His face looked straight at me from close by and with penetrating force, and he whispered in my ear, 'Remember me so that you may know me when I meet you.' When I came to, his image had not slipped from my mind. How greatly was I distracted from him by work for a time and by fun for a time, and yet he returns with all his force as though he had not been absent for a single moment. Under the pressure of anxiety, I ask myself: When will he meet me? How does the meeting take place? And what is the reason for all this? It is seldom that I drive out apprehensions, even in warm embraces.[213]

Echoes of an Autobiography

Time, never a force of good in the individual's life in Mahfouz's world, deals its ultimate cruelty in its final manifestation as Death, the cessation of time, as it were, for the individual. Ever a major preoccupation of the author's, it becomes an obsessive thought in his old age and dominates a great many of the parabolic narratives of *Echoes of an Autobiography*.

Dominant too is a sense of bewilderment before the enigma of existence, of awe before the harshness of the world, and a pitiable longing for deliverance answered only by the indifferent silence of the Unknown, as in the story 'The Postman': 'On one of the nights of the cave there was a strong wind and a heavy outpour of rain. Gusts of air penetrating through from the entrance played with the wispy flames of the candles, and hearts beat violently. Eyes were directed at the entrance and they waited, hearts beating even more wildly. One of them whispered, "They say that the night of this year is

Mahfouz receiving the Order of the Nile from President Mubarak in 1988

blessed." Hearts were drawn towards the entrance with all the strength they possessed. A whistling came to them from afar and they jumped to their feet. At that moment the postman entered in his familiar uniform and with his bag, almost drenched from the water soaking his clothes. Calmly he gave to each outstretched hand a letter, then left without uttering a word. They broke open the envelopes and looked at the letters by the light of the candles. They found that they were blank pieces of paper with nothing on them.' Abd-Rabbih exclaimed, "The outcome will be known to those who are patient."[214]

The new form of the aphoristic narrative or parable that Mahfouz introduced in *Echoes of an Autobiography* was sustained in the following years with some variance in the creations known as the 'Dreams' which he continued to write virtually until his death. (Interestingly, Mahfouz has rejected comparisons with the Japanese *haiku* poem on the basis that Japanese poets wrote *haiku* out of choice, while he was forced to invent that genre because he could not in his old age and frail health muster the energy to write anything longer.[215]) Composed over a number of years (2000–06) and serialised in the Cairene magazine *Nisf al-dunya*, the dreams first appeared in English translation in 2004 as *The Dreams* (with a sequel in 2007 as *Dreams of Departure*) before they were published in book form in Arabic in 2006, shortly before the author's death. (According to one account, Mahfouz never saw the book, as he had already fallen into his final coma when a first copy was brought to his bedside in hospital.[216]) One basic difference between the narratives of *Echoes of an Autobiography* and those of *The Dreams* is in the manner of composition. According to Mahfouz, the former despite their own oneiric quality are conscious inventions, while the latter are mostly based on actual dreams or nightmares which he recollected and composed into prose with varying measures of interference: *The texts I write under the rubric of 'Dreams of the Period of Convalescence' represent some dreams as I saw them, fragments of dreams that I saw and enlarged, as well as imagined dreams.*[217] This quality also distinguishes them from an earlier set of dreams included in a short story collection of 1982 by the title *Ra'aytu fi ma yara al-na'im* or 'I Saw in a Dream'. Those too, the author affirms, were made up, not genuine dreams.[218] Mahfouz's statements distinguishing

> This is a trial and this a bench and sitting at it is a single judge and this is the seat of the accused and sitting at it is a group of national leaders and this is the courtroom, where I sat down longing to get to know the party responsible for what has befallen us. But I grow confused when the dialogue between the judge and the leaders is conducted in a language I have never before heard, until the magistrate adjusts himself in his seat as he prepares to announce the verdict in the Arabic tongue. I lean forward to hear, but then the judge points at me – to pronounce a sentence of death upon me. I cry out in alarm that I'm not part of this proceeding and that I'd come of my own free will simply to watch and see – but no one even notices my scream.
>
> 'Dream 100' from *The Dreams*

Echoes of an Autobiography from *The Dreams* are largely upheld by the reading of the two texts. I say 'largely' because the conscious artist, preoccupied with the message, can never be entirely away from the work of Mahfouz, as for instance in 'Dream 100', clearly 'structured' as a 'dream' to give a familiar Mahfouzian moral lesson: to seek personal safety in remaining aloof from political or social strife is a false hope.

However, the presence of the absurd, surreal or irrational in *The Dreams* is of such prevalence and power that a substantial number of the narratives actually appear mostly without design and resistant to interpretation with any certainty if at all. By contrast, elements of the absurd or surreal in *Echoes of an Autobiography* are clearly consciously managed and will yield on investigation perfectly rational meaning in line with the author's known intellectual preoccupations. Mahfouz's history with the absurd,

I saw myself in Abbasiya wandering in the vastness of my memories, recalling in particular the late Lady A. so I contacted her by telephone, inviting her to meet me by the fountain, and there I welcomed her with a passionate heart. I suggested that we spend the evening together in Fishawi Café, as in our happiest days. But when we reached the familiar place, the deceased blind bookseller came over to us and greeted us warmly – though he scolded the dearly departed A for her long absence. She told him what had kept her away was Death. But he rejected that excuse – for Death, he said, can never come between those who love and their loved ones.

'Dream 104' from *The Dreams*[219]

surreal and expressionist is by no means a matter of his last years. In fact, it goes back a long way, to the years 1969–73 when in the aftermath of the 1967 Arab defeat in the war with Israel, he broke into a frenzied period of short story and one-act play writing that severed itself from realism and gave in to the surreal dictates of the subconscious. Or seemed to do so, I should say, since behind the surrealist façade the strict Mahfouzian discipline with its permissibility of rational interpretation was discernible. Not so *The Dreams*, which rely for effect on pathos, on the feelings of pity or

The statue of Mahfouz erected in 2003 in Sphinx Square in Cairo, not far from his home

fear they create, on the sense of mystery and enchantment and the sheer poetry of the language, rather than any logical sense, apparent or deducible. *The Dreams* therefore will probably always stand out as a Mahfouzian indulgence that he allowed himself in old age: the disciplinarian craftsman, who always kept a tight grip on his art matter, for once let go.

Notes

1. Jamal al-Ghitani, *Naguib Mahfouz yatadhakkar*, Introduction to 3rd edition (Cairo: 1987?) p 22, hereafter Ghitani, *Mahfouz yatadhakkar*.
2. Ghitani, *Mahfouz yatadhakkar*, p 107.
3. Ghitani, *Mahfouz yatadhakkar*, pp 46–7.
4. Ghitani, *Mahfouz yatadhakkar*, pp 120–1.
5. See interview in *al-Musawwar*, 21 October 1988, pp 10–19, 68–73.
6. Ghitani, *Mahfouz yatadhakkar*, p 126.
7. Ghitani, *Mahfouz yatadhakkar*, p 47.
8. Ghitani, *Mahfouz yatadhakkar*, pp 16, 52
9. *Mirrors,* p 45.
10. Ghitani, *Mahfouz yatadhakkar*, pp 52, 101, 106; see also Mahfouz, *Atahaddath ilaykum* (Beirut: 1977) pp 78–80, hereafter *Atahaddath ilaykum*.
11. Ghitani, *Mahfouz yatadhakkar*, pp 45–6.
12. Ghitani, *Mahfouz yatadhakkar*, pp 49–50, 153.
13. See *al-Hilal*, February 1970, pp 98–9.
14. *Atahaddath ilaykum*, pp 80–1.
15. *Atahaddath ilaykum*, pp 79, 84.
16. Ghitani, *Mahfouz yatadhakkar*, pp 49, 52–3, 153.
17. A translation of this story is included in Naguib Mahfouz, *The Time and the Place and Other Stories.*
18. Ghitani, *Mahfouz yatadhakkar*, p 58.

19. *Whispers of Madness.* The Arabic title of the story is 'Hulm Saʿa'.

20. *Mirrors,* pp 210–12, 214.

21. Ghitani, *Mahfouz yatadhakkar*, p 49.

22. *Fountain and Tomb*, Tale 6.

23. *Fountain and Tomb*, Tales 4–7, 10, 17, 24, and 25.

24. *Fountain and Tomb*, pp 43–4.

25. Ghitani, *Mahfouz yatadhakkar*, pp 60–1.

26. Fu'ad Dawwara, *Naguib Mahfouz min al-qawmiyya ila al-ʿalamiyya* (Naguib Mahfouz from National to International Fame) (Cairo: 1989) pp 211–12, hereafter Dawwara, *Naguib Mahfouz.*

27. Interview in *al-Adab*, July 1960; quoted in Sasson Somekh, *The Changing Rhythm* (Leiden: 1973) pp 37–8.

28. Ghitani, *Mahfouz yatadhakkar*, p 77.

29. From an interview in *al-Majalla,* January 1963; quoted in Somekh, *The Changing Rhythm*, p 38.

30. Ghitani, *Mahfouz yatadhakkar*, p 62.

31. Dawwara, *Naguib Mahfouz*, p 212.

32. Ibrahim Mansur, *al-Izdiwaj al-thaqafi wa azmat al-muʿarada al-misriyya* (Cultural Dichotomy and the Predicament of Egyptian Opposition) (Beirut: 1981) p 86, hereafter Mansur, *al-Izdiwaj al-thaqafi.*

33. Dawwara, *Naguib Mafouz*, p 212.

34. *Atahaddath ilaykum*, pp 87–8.

35. See ʿAbd al-Muhsin Taha Badr, *al-Ruʾya wa-l-adat* (Vision and Technique) (Cairo: 1978) pp 33–72 for a review of the articles, and pp 489–93 for a bibliographic list.

36. Badr, *al-Ruʾya wa-l-adat*, pp 46–8.

37. See pp 66–7 for a fuller quotation of Mahfouz's views of time.

38. See Bergson in the *Encyclopaedia Britannica*.

39. Ghitani, *Mahfouz yatadhakkar*, p 75.

40. In the following pages I have drawn heavily on the many interviews contained in Mahfouz's *Atahaddath ilaykum,* in addition to Dawwara's *Naguib Mahfouz* and Ghitani's *Mahfouz yatadhakkar.* Where I feel a more specific reference is needed, one will be given.

41. *Atahaddath ilaykum*, pp 94–5.

42. Dawwara, *Naguib Mahfouz*, pp 213–14.

43. *Atahaddath ilaykum*, pp 52, 154, 161–2.

44. *Atahaddath ilaykum*, pp 95–6; see also Ghitani, *Mahfouz yatadhakkar*, p 110.

45. Ghitani, *Mahfouz yatadhakkar*, pp 93–4.

46. *Atahaddath ilaykum*, p 95.

47. Ghitani, *Mahfouz yatadhakkar*, pp 80, 100–01.

48. *Atahaddath ilaykum*, p 72.

49. Ghitani, *Mahfouz yatadhakkar*, p 80.

50. Dawwara, *Naguib Mahfouz*, p 226; see also *Atahaddath ilaykum,* p 96.

51. For an English translation see, Taha Husayn (trans. Sidney Galzer), *The Future of Culture in Egypt* (Octagon Books, New York: 1975).

52. Mansur, *al-Izdiwaj al-thaqafi*, pp 90–1.

53. Interview in *al-Qabas*, 11 June 1987.

54. Ghitani, *Mahfouz yatadhakkar*, p 117.

55. *Atahaddath ilaykum*, p 32. For some recreations of those violent scenes see *Mirrors*, sketches of 'Badr al-Ziyadi' and 'Taha Enan'.

56. Ghitani, *Mahfouz yatadhakkar*, p 118.

57. See the sketch of 'Abd al-Wahab Ismail' (the fictitious name Mahfouz gives Qutb) in *Mirrors*, pp 261–7; see also *Al-Hilal*, December 1988, pp 98–101 for confirmation of this interpretation of the character.

58. *Atahaddath ilaykum*, pp 16–17

59. Ghitani, *Mahfouz yatadhakkar*, p 98.

60. Ghali Shukri, *al-Muntami* (The Nonconformist) (2nd edition, Cairo: 1969) p 239; see also Dawwara, *Naguib Mahfouz*, p 227; Ghitani, *Mahfouz yatadhakkar*, p 138; interview by George Tarabishi in *Anwal,* 31 March 1989, p 15; *Atahaddath ilaykum*, p 91.

61. Shukri, *al-Muntami*, p 239.

62. *Atahaddath ilaykum*, pp 98–9.

63. *Mirrors*, p 250.

64. The Charter for National Action, the political manifesto of the state presented by Nasser to the nation in 1962.

65. *Mirrors*, p 345.

66. See for example *Atahaddath ilaykum*, p 204.

67. Interview by George Tarabishi in *Anwal*, 31 March 1989, pp 15, 21.

68. For information used in this section I have drawn on the following sources in order of importance: Ghitani, *Mahfouz yatadhakkar*; *Atahaddath ilaykum*; Adham Rajab, 'Safahat majhula min hayat Naguib Mahfouz' (Unknown Chapters from the Life of Naguib Mahfouz); and Muhammad 'Afifi, 'Naguib Mahfouz rajul al-sa'a' (Naguib Mahfouz, Man of the Clock) – both in *al-Hilal*, February 1970, pp 92–9 and 137–41, respectively.

69. This count does not include such works as the collected interviews (*Atahaddath ilaykum*), or the memoirs (*Naguib Mahfouz yatadhakkar*), as the first was selected and introduced by Sabri Hafiz, while the second was prepared by Jamal al-Ghitani from conversations with Mahfouz. On the other hand, a work difficult to classify, *Before the Throne*, has been counted, for convenience's sake, as a novel.

70. This produced the short story 'Three Days in Yemen' about Egyptian soldiers at war in Yemen (1962–7). The story is included in the collection *Under the Bus Shelter* (1969).

71. *Palace of Desire*, p 195.

72. Ghitani, *Mahfouz yatadhakkar*, pp 25–6.

73. Interview by George Tarabishi in *Anwal,* 31 March 1989, p 15.

74. For Mahfouz's own account of the effects of the attack on his life, see his *Reflections of a Nobel Laureate*, pp 8–20.

75. This period of Mahfouz's life is documented in Gamal al-Ghitani's *al-Majalis al-mahfuziya* (Cairo: 2006), hereafter Ghitani, *al-Majalis*. For an English translation, see Gamal al-Ghitani, *The Mahfouz Dialogs*, trans. Humphrey Davies, (AUC Press, Cairo: 2007). All references however are to the Arabic original.

76. For a painful account of Mahfouz's last three weeks in hospital, his funeral and burial, see Muhammad Salmawi, *Naguib Mahfouz: al-mahatta al-akhira* (Cairo: 2006). For an English translation, see Mohamed Salmawy, *The Last Station: Naguib Mahfouz Looking Back*, trans. Andy Smart and Nadia Fouda-Smart (AUC Press, Cairo: 2007).

77. Mahfouz gives 1932 in the list of publications usually appended to his books. However, Fatima Musa quotes 1931 as the date indicated on the index of the Egyptian National Library. See her *Fi-l-riwaya al-'arabiyya al-mu'asira* (On the Contemporary Arabic Novel) (Cairo: 1972?) p 35, hereafter Fatima Musa, *Fi-l-riwaya al-'arabiyya*.

78. See Somekh, *The Changing Rhythm*, p 42, fn 1.

79. Naguib Mahfouz (trans), *Misr al-qadima* (Ancient Egypt) (Cairo: 1931?; reprinted Cairo: 1988).

80. Ali Shalash, *Naguib Mahfouz: al-tariq wa-l-sada* (Naguib Mahfouz: the Road and the Echo) (Beirut: 1990) p 40.

81. Fatima Musa, *Fi-l-riwaya al-'arabiyya*, p 35.

82. *Echoes of an Autobiography*, trans D Johnson-Davies, p 31.

83. *Atahaddath ilaykum*, p 92.

84. *Before the Throne*, pp 197, 198.

85. *Before the Throne*, p 198.

86. *Atahaddath ilaykum*, p 90.

87. Ghali Shukri, *Naguib Mahfouz: min al-Jamaliyya ila Nobel* (Naguib Mahfouz: from Jamaliyya to Nobel) (Cairo: 1988) p 70, hereafter Shukri, *Naguib Mahfouz*.

88. The dates of publication given by Mahfouz for his first two social novels, *Khan al-Khalili* and *Cairo Modern*, are not reliable. Sasson Somekh was probably the first scholar to draw attention to this fact. Contrary to Mahfouz's account which reverses the order and dates, he established that *Khan al-Khalili* was Mahfouz's first realistic novel, published in 1945, followed in 1946 by *Cairo Modern*. See Somekh, *The Changing Rhythm*, pp 198–9.

89. *Khan al-Khalili*, p 8.

90. *Khan al-Khalili*, p 55.

91. *Cairo Modern*, p 25.

92. *Cairo Modern*, p 26.

93. *Cairo Modern*, p 9.

94. *Cairo Modern*, pp 12–13.

95. *Midaq Alley*, p 178.

96. *The Mirage* was published one year after *Midaq Alley*. Mahfouz, however, has said that it pre-dated the latter in writing and that it was the success of *Midaq Alley* that encouraged him to publish it. *Midaq Alley* being a more accomplished work, this argument would seem to make sense. See Fatima Musa, *Fi-l-riwaya al-ʿarabiyya*, p 43.

97. *The Mirage*, p 8.

98. *The Beginning and the End*, p 184.

99. *The Beginning and the End*, p 32.

100. *Atahaddath ilaykum*, p 153.

101. *The Beginning and the End*, p 381.

102. *The Beginning and the End*, p 283.

103. *The Beginning and the End*, p 381.

104. *The Beginning and the End*, p 302.

105. *The Beginning and the End*, p 180.

106. *Atahaddath ilaykum*, pp 150–1, 46, 173–4.

107. Ghitani, *Mahfouz yatadhakkar*, pp 98–9; Ghali Shukri, *Naguib Mahfouz*, pp 105–6, 133.

108. An exception is *The Return of the Spirit* (1933) by Tawfiq al-Hakim (trans. William M Hutchins (Three Continents Press, Washington D.C.: 1990)), but it does so on a much smaller scale than *The Trilogy*.

109. *Palace Walk*, p 483.

110. *Sugar Street*, p 393.

111. *Palace Walk*, p 24.

112. *Palace of Desire*, p 34.

113. *Palace of Desire*, p 183.

114. *Palace of Desire*, p 45.

115. *Sugar Street*, p 6.

116. *Atahaddath ilaykum*, p 157.

117. *Palace of Desire*, Chapter 33, *passim*.

118. *Palace of Desire*, p 410.

119. *Palace of Desire*, p 412.

120. *Palace of Desire*, p 412.

121. *Palace of Desire*, p 413.

122. *Sugar Street*, p 264.

123. *Palace Walk*, p 43.

124. *Palace Walk*, p 7.

125. *Atahaddath ilaykum*, p 62.

126. *Palace of Desire*, p 372.

127. *Palace of Desire*, p 22.

128. *Palace of Desire*, p 23.

129. *Palace of Desire*, p 217.

130. Here are some examples. On first hearing his name uttered by her lips, Kamal feels like crying out '*Zammiluni! Daththiruni!*' (Wrap me up! Cover me with my mantle!) (*Palace of Desire*, p 22) – the famous words attributed to the

Prophet Muhammad, who felt feverish after first receiving the Revelation from Gabriel (in the Koran the Prophet is referred to as the '*Muzzammil*' and the '*Muddaththir*' (see the opening verses of *Suras* LXXIII and LXXIV)). He also refers to the house of the Shaddads where she lives as '*manzil al-wahy wa mab'ath al-sana*" (the place where revelation descended and light emanated) (*Palace of Desire*, p 26) – stock phrases again associated with the history of the Prophet. Elsewhere Kamal draws an image from the Gospels, referring to an event which pre-dated the beginning of his love for Aïda as having occurred 'before the Holy Spirit had descended on him' (*Palace of Desire*, p 81).

131. *Sugar Street*, p 227.

132. *Palace Walk*, p 462.

133. *Palace Walk*, p 559.

134. *Sugar Street*, pp 44–5.

135. *Children of the Alley*, p 503.

136. *Children of the Alley*, p 538.

137. *Children of the Alley*, p 483.

138. *Atahaddath ilaykum*, p 91; see also Ghitani, *Mahfouz yatadhakkar,* p 138.

139. Interview in *al-Qabas*, 31 December 1975; quoted in Ibrahim al-Shaykh, *Mawaqif ijtima'iyya wa siyasiyya fi adab Naguib Mahfouz* (Social and Political Positions in the Writing of Naguib Mahfouz) (3rd edition, Cairo: 1987) p 164.

140. The story of Said Mahran was inspired by a real-life criminal by the name of Mahmoud Amin Sulayman, who also believed that his wife was unfaithful to him and was out to get her. His story, which captured the public imagination in 1960, was extensively covered by the press. He gave the police a hard time until he was chased down

with the help of police dogs to a cave near Hilwan where he fought to the death. Mahfouz was admittedly greatly moved by the incident and within months he had written his novel. See *Atahaddath ilaykum,* pp 112–13; Ghitani, *Mahfouz yatadhakkar*, p 108; Yahya Haqqi, *'Itr al-ahbab*, p 113; Fatima Musa, *Bayna adabayn* (Between Two Literatures) (Cairo: 1965) pp 132–5.

141. *Atahaddath ilaykum*, p 156.
142. Notably Ghali Shukri throughout his study of Mahfouz, *al-Muntami*.
143. From interview with Mahfouz in Ahmad Hashim al-Sharif, *Naguib Mahfouz: muhawarat qabla Nobel* (Naguib Mahfouz: Conversations before Nobel) (Cairo: 1989) pp 29–30.
144. *The Thief and the Dogs*, pp 89–90.
145. *The Thief and the Dogs*, p 125.
146. *The Beggar*, p 45.
147. See 'Existentialism' in J A Cuddon, *The Penguin Dictionary of Literary Terms and Literary Theories* (London: 1999).
148. *Adrift on the Nile*, p 56.
149. *Adrift on the Nile*, p 55.
150. An allusion to the Egyptian military campaign in Yemen (1962–7).
151. A reference to the revolution's *nouveaux riches*, who inherited the privileges of the regime they ousted.
152. *Adrift on the Nile*, p 126.
153. Quoted in Shukri, *Naguib Mahfouz*, p 56.
154. *Adrift on the Nile*, p 199.
155. Translated into English by Desmond Stewart (London: 1966).
156. *Atahaddath ilaykum*, p 111.
157. Interview in *al-Fikr al-mu'asir,* December 1966, p 112, quoted in Somekh, *The Changing Rhythm*, p 187.
158. Ghitani, *Mahfouz yatadhakkar*, pp 108–9.

159. *Mirrors*, p 413.
160. *Atahaddath ilaykum*, pp 78–9.
161. Ghitani, *al-Majalis*, p 96.
162. *Fountain and Tomb*, p 4.
163. *Fountain and Tomb*, p 5.
164. *Fountain and Tomb*, p 189.
165. *Harafish*, p 11.
166. *Harafish*, p 12.
167. *Harafish*, p 12.
168. *Harafish*, p 19.
169. *Harafish*, pp 61–2.
170. *Harafish*, p 71.
171. *Harafish*, p 85.
172. *Harafish*, p 383.
173. *Harafish*, p 387.
174. *Harafish*, p 404.
175. *Harafish*, p 405.
176. *Harafish*, p 420.
177. *Harafish*, p 412.
178. *Harafish*, pp 422–3.
179. *Harafish*, p 431.
180. *Harafish*, pp 435–6.
181. *Harafish*, pp 554–5.
182. *Harafish*, p 514.
183. *Harafish*, p 531.
184. *Harafish*, p 519.
185. *Harafish*, p 87.
186. *Harafish*, p 567.
187. *Arabian Nights and Days*, p 261.
188. See *Rihlat Ibn Battuta* (Beirut: 1964) p 4.
189. *The Journey of Ibn Fattouma*, p 5.
190. *The Journey of Ibn Fattouma*, p 18.
191. *The Journey of Ibn Fattouma*, p 19.

192. See *Ibn Battuta: Travels in Asia and Africa*, trans and selected with introduction and notes by H A R Gibb (London: 1929) p 4.

193. Mahmud Amin al-'Alim, *Ta'mmulat fi'alam Naguib Mahfouz* (Reflections on the World of Naguib Mahfouz) (Cairo: 1970) p 139.

194. For a complete list, see Badr, *al-Ru'ya wa-l-adat*, pp 494–8.

195. The controversy over the publication date is complex and was caused by the date of 1938 given by Mahfouz but established beyond doubt by researchers (and subsequently admitted by Mahfouz) to be a few years earlier than the true date. For details of the controversy, see my fuller study of Mahfouz, *Naguib Mahfouz: the Pursuit of Meaning* (Routledge, London and New York: 1993) p 246, fns 6–10.

196. It must be noted that the anthology in translation by the same title is not a full translation of Mahfouz's *Dunya Allah* (i.e. God's World). In fact it is a representative selection, which spans no less than six collections by the author.

197. Ghitani, *al-Majalis*, pp 90–1; see also interview with Yusuf al-Qa'id in *al-Hayat*, 12 April 1990.

198. For an English translation, see *The Time and the Place*.

199. For a good critique of this story, see Sasson Somekh, 'Za'balawi' – Author, Theme and Technique', *Journal of Arabic Literature*, vol 1 (1970) pp 24–35.

200. Dawwara, *Naguib Mahfouz*, p 240.

201. *Atahaddath ilaykum*, pp 210–11.

202. *Atahaddath ilaykum*, p 179.

203. *Atahaddath ilaykum*, p 182.

204. For a translation of this story and five others from the same collection, see *The Time and the Place*.

205. *The Final Decision*, p 5.

206. *The Final Decision*, pp 94–5.

207. *Sada al-nisyan* (Maktabat Misr, Cairo: 1999) p 69.

208. *Qushtumur Café*, p 5.

209. The Arabic title for *The Dreams* is *Ahlam fatrat al-naqaha*, which literally translates as 'Dreams of the Period of Convalescence', a title probably inspired by the start of their composition in the years following the attempt on Mahfouz's life in 1994. *The Dreams* started being published in the Cairo weekly women's magazine *Nisf al-Dunya* in 2000 and continued until Mahfouz's death in 2006, published in book form in Arabic only in that year. The English translations by Raymond Stock were published in two volumes by the American University in Cairo Press in 2004 and 2007 as *The Dreams* and *Dreams of Departure*, respectively.

210. *Reflections of a Nobel Laureate: 1994–2001*, p 61.

211. Ghitani, *al-Majalis*, p 305

212. *Echoes of an Autobiography*, trans D Johnson-Davies, p 13.

213. *Echoes of an Autobiography*, p 71.

214. *Echoes of an Autobiography*, p 88.

215. *Reflections of a Nobel Laureate*, p 77.

216. Salmawi, *al-Mahatta al-akhira*, pp 43, 68 and 75–6.

217. Ghitani, *al-Majalis*, p 54.

218. Ghitani, *al-Majalis*, pp 90–1.

219. Raymond Stock's translation of 'Dream 104' is slightly modified by me in line with the Arabic; see *The Dreams*.

Year	Age	Life
1911		11 December: Naguib Mahfouz born in the Jamaliyya quarter of Cairo.
1919	8	Witnesses 1919 revolution in wake of arrest and exile of Saad Zaghloul.
1924	13	Mahfouz and his family move from Jamaliyya to the Cairo suburb of Abbasiyya.
1930	19	Enters King Fuad I University to study philosophy.
1931	20	Publishes translation of James Baikie's *Ancient Egypt*.
1934	23	Graduates from university. Joins civil service, and takes clerical post at Cairo University.

Year	History	Culture
1911	Assassination of Egyptian Prime Minister Boutros Ghali Pasha. Agadir Crisis. Outbreak of Italo-Turkish War.	D H Lawrence, *The White Peacock*.
1919	Versailles Peace Conference. Allenby appointed British High Commissioner in Egypt. April: Zaghloul and colleagues released. December: Milner mission arrives in Egypt.	Thomas Hardy, *Collected Poems*.
1924	January: Wafd Party wins first election. September: Abortive negotiations for a treaty. November: Assassination of Governor-General of the Sudan leads to Zaghloul's resignation.	E M Forster, *A Passage to India*. Film: *The Ten Commandments*.
1930	Last Allied troops leave the Rhineland. Naval Disarmament Treaty.	Evelyn Waugh, *Vile Bodies*. Films: *The Blue Angel*; *Anna Christie*.
1931	Britain abandons Gold Standard. Second National Government in Britain.	Films: *City Lights* (Chaplin); *Frankenstein*.
1934	'Night of the Long Knives' in Germany. In Soviet Union, assassination of Kirov triggers Stalin's purges.	F Scott Fitzgerald, *Tender is the Night*. Robert Graves, *I, Claudius* and *Claudius the God*. Film: *The Thin Man*; *The Private Life of Henry VIII*.

Year	Age	Life
1938	27	Moves to Ministry of Religious Endowments as parliamentary secretary to the minister.
1939	28	Publishes his first novel, *Khufu's Wisdom*.
1945	34	Requests transfer to the al-Ghuri Library in Jamaliyya and administers Good Loan Project. Publishes first 'realistic' novel *Khan al-Khalili*.
1952	41	Mahfouz finishes writing *The Cairo Trilogy* and stops writing for five years following the Free Officers' revolution. Begins work in a series of cultural posts, until his retirement.
1954	43	Marries Atiyyatallah Ibrahim.

Year	History	Culture
1938	Nahas Pasha dismissed as Prime Minister of Egypt by King Farouk.	Graham Greene, *Brighton Rock*. Films: *Alexander Nevski*; *Pygmalion*.
1939	Outbreak of Second World War.	James Joyce, *Finnegan's Wake*. C S Forester, *Captain Horatio Hornblower*. Film: *Gone with the Wind*; *The Wizard of Oz*.
1945	End of Second World War.	George Orwell, *Animal Farm*. Evelyn Waugh, *Brideshead Revisited*. Films: *Rome, Open City*; *Brief Encounter*.
1952	January: Widespread anti-British activity. July: Free Officers overthrow government; General Naguib becomes leader; King Farouk deposed. December: Repeal of 1923 constitution and dissolution of political parties.	F R Leavis, *The Common Pursuit*. Film: *High Noon*.
1954	March: Naguib overthrown and replaced by Nasser. October: British agree to evacuation of Egypt; assassination attempt on Nasser leads to mass arrests of Muslim Brotherhood.	Thomas Mann, *Felix Krull*. J R R Tolkien, *The Lord of the Rings*. Films: *On the Waterfront*; *The Seven Samurai*.

Year	Age	Life
1956	45	*Cairo Trilogy* published (to 1957).
1959	48	*al-Ahram* newspaper serialises *Children of the Alley*.
1967	56	After Six-Day War, writes no novels for five years, but many short stories.
1970	59	Death of Nasser, who is succeeded by Sadat.
1971	60	Retires from the civil service. Invited to be writer emeritus at *al-Ahram* newspaper.
1973	62	Yom Kippur War: Initial Egyptian successes do much to restore national morale.

Year	History	Culture
1956	June: Withdrawal of last British troops from Egypt. July: President Nasser announces nationalisation of Suez Canal after US and Britain renege on loan offer. October: Israel invades Sinai. November: British and French landings at Suez; Egyptians blockade canal. December: British and French troops forced to withdraw.	John Osborne, *Look Back in Anger*. Film: *The Seventh Seal*.
1959	Castro comes to power in Cuba. Britain and United Arab Republic restore diplomatic relations.	James Michener, *Hawaii*. Ian Fleming, *Goldfinger*. Films: *La Dolce Vita*; *Ben Hur*.
1967	Arab defeat in Six-Day War with Israel.	Gore Vidal, *Washington DC*. Ira Levin, *Rosemary's Baby*. Films: *Blow-Up*; *Bonnie and Clyde*.
1970	United Arab Republic and Israel agree to 99-day truce along Suez Canal. Kent State shootings.	Iris Murdoch, *A Fairly Honourable Defeat*. John Mortimer, *A Voyage Round My Father*. Films: *Paint Your Wagon*; *True Grit*.
1971	US bombing of Cambodia. Indo-Pakistan War.	E M Forster, *Maurice*. Herman Wouk, *The Winds of War*. Films: *A Clockwork Orange*; *The French Connection*.
1973	Watergate scandal. Ceasefire in Vietnam War.	Thomas Pynchon, *Gravity's Rainbow*. Film: *Last Tango in Paris*.

Year	Age	Life
1981	70	Assassination of Sadat at military parade by Muslim extremists. He is succeeded by Hosni Mubarak.
1987	76	Last novel, *Qushtumur Café*, published.
1988	77	Nobel Prize for Literature. Awarded Order of the Nile by Egyptian government.
1989	78	Awarded Presidential Medal from the American University in Cairo. Joins 80 Arab intellectuals in statement against Rushdie *fatwa*.
1991	80	Travels to London for heart surgery.
1992	81	Elected honorary member of the American Academy and Institute of Arts and Letters.

Year	History	Culture
1981	Israel formally annexes the Golan Heights.	Salman Rushdie, *Midnight's Children*. William Boyd, *A Good Man in Africa*. Films: *On Golden Pond*; *Time Bandits*.
1987	US President Reagan visits Berlin. Margaret Thatcher elected British Prime Minister for the third time.	Ian McEwan, *The Child in Time*. Tom Wolfe, *The Bonfire of the Vanities*. Films: *Cry Freedom*; *Wall Street*.
1988	Palestinian 'Intifada' begins in Occupied Territories. Soviet troops begin retreat from Afghanistan.	Gabriel Garcia Marquez, *Love in the Time of Cholera*. Salman Rushdie, *The Satanic Verses*. Film: *A Fish Called Wanda*; *Rain Man*.
1989	Last Soviet troops leave Afghanistan. Fatwa by Iranian leader Ayatollah Khomeini against Salman Rushdie for *The Satanic Verses*.	Kazuo Ishiguro, *The Remains of the Day*. Umberto Eco, *Foucault's Pendulum*. Films: *Driving Miss Daisy*; *Steel Magnolias*.
1991	Operation Desert Storm: Coalition forces liberate Kuwait from Iraqi occupation. Warsaw Pact officially dissolved.	Pat Barker, *Regeneration*. Films: *JFK*; *Cape Fear*.
1992	Break-up of Yugoslavia begins.	Michael Ondaatje, *The English Patient*. Iain Banks, *The Crow Road*. Films: *Howards End*; *The Player*.

Year	Age	Life
1994	83	14 October: Assassination attempt by Muslim extremist after *fatwa* condemning *Children of the Alley* for blasphemy.
1995	84	Awarded honorary doctorate by the American University in Cairo.
2002	91	Elected to the American Academy of Arts and Sciences.
2006	94	30 August: Dies in hospital just as last book, *Dreams of Convalescence*, is published in Arabic. 31 August: State funeral with full military honours.

Year	History	Culture
1994	Channel Tunnel opens. Nelson Mandela inaugurated as South Africa's first black president.	Alan Hollinghurst, *The Folding Star*. Film: *The Madness of King George*.
1995	Oklahoma City bombing in USA. NATO begins bombing of Serbian positions in Bosnia.	Frank McCourt, *Angela's Ashes*. Nelson Mandela, *Long Walk to Freedom*. Films: *Apollo 13*; *Twelve Monkeys*.
2002	US invasion of Afghanistan. Death of Queen Elizabeth the Queen Mother.	R Mistry, *Family Matters*. Film: *One Hour Photo*.
2006	Israel invades Lebanon in attack on Hezbollah.	John Updike, *Terrorist*. Film: *The Da Vinci Code*.

The Works of Naguib Mahfouz

In the following list I begin with the Arabic title in italics followed by its English rendering. To avoid confusion, where there are published translations I have adopted their titles and italicised them. The first date given is that of first publication in Arabic in book form. No account is taken of newspaper or magazine serialisation dates (very common with the work of Mahfouz after *The Cairo Trilogy*). Publication in book form usually came within a year after serialisation, except in the case of *Children of the Alley* (serialised in 1959, book in 1967). A few of the first publication dates given (indicated with an asterisk) will contradict the dates authorised by Mahfouz. The reasons for adopting different dates can be found in the appropriate sections of this book where such works are discussed. The second column of dates lists in brackets the dates of Arabic editions used in this study. It is to those editions that my page references are made. Where there is an uncertainty about a date, it will be followed by a question mark. Where the edition used is the first published, the second column will be left blank. Unless otherwise indicated, the place of publication is Cairo. Translations of quotations from the Arabic texts are in most, but not all, cases my own.

The Novels

'*Abath al-aqdar*	*Khufu's Wisdom*	1939	(1982)
Radubis	*Rhadopis of Nubia*	1943	(1947?)
Kifah Tiba	*Thebes at War*	1944	(n.d.)
Khan al-Khalili	Khan al-Khalili	1945*	(1960)
al-Qahira al-jadida	*Cairo Modern*	1946*	(1974)
Zuqaq al-Madaqq	*Midaq Alley*	1947	(1972)
al-Sarab	The Mirage	1948	(1982)
Bidaya wa nihaya	*The Beginning and the End*	1949	(1973)
al-Thulathiya	*The Cairo Trilogy*		
1 *Bayn al-qasrayn*	*Palace Walk*	1956	(1970)
2 *Qasr al-shawq*	*Palace of Desire*	1957	(n.d.)
3 *al-Sukkariya*	*Sugar Street*	1957	(1971?)
Awlad haratina (Beirut)	*Children of the Alley*	(1967)	(1972)
al-Liss wa-l-kilab	*The Thief and the Dogs*	1961	(n.d.)
al-Summan wa-l-kharif	*Autumn Quail*	1962	(n.d.)
al-Tariq	*The Search*	1964	(1965)
al-Shahhadh	*The Beggar*	1965	(1978)
Tharthara fawq al-Nil	*Adrift on the Nile*	1966	(1973)
Miramar	*Miramar*	1967	(1976)
al-Maraya	*Mirrors*	1972	
al-Hubb taht al-matar	Love in the Rain	1973	
al-Karnak	*Karnak Café*	1974	
Hadrat al-muhtaram	*Respected Sir*	1975	
Hikayat haratina	*Fountain and Tomb*	1975	
Qalb al-layl	Heart of the Night	1975	
Malhamat al-harafish	*The Harafish*	1977	
'*Asr al-hubb*	The Age of Love	1980	
Afrah al-qubba	*Wedding Song*	1981	
Layali alf layla	*Arabian Nights and Days*	1982	

al-Baqi min al-zaman sa'a	There only Remains an Hour	1982
Rihlat Ibn Fattuma	*The Journey of Ibn Fattouma*	1983
Amam al-'arsh	Before the Throne	1983
Yawm qutila al-za'im	*The Day the Leader was Killed*	1985
al-'A'ish fi-l-haqiqa	*Akhenaten: Dweller in Truth*	1985
Hadith al-sabah wa-l-masa'	*Morning and Evening Talk*	1987
Qushtumur	Qushtumur Café	1988

Collected Short Stories
(Titles of collections including plays are followed by the number of plays they contain between brackets.)

Hams al-junun	Whispers of Madness	1948?*	(1973)
Dunya Allah	God's World	1963	(1973)
Bayt sayyi' al-sum'a	A House of Ill Repute	1965	(1974?)
Khammarat al-qitt al-aswad	The Black Cat Tavern	1969	(1974)
Taht al-mazalla (5)	Under the Bus Shelter	1969	(1974)
Hikaya bila bidaya wala nihaya	A Tale without Beginning or End	1971	(1973)
Shahr al-'asal	The Honeymoon	1971	(1973)
al-Jarima (1)	The Crime	1973	
al-Hubb fawq hadabat al-haram	Love under the Pyramids	1979	
al-Shaytan ya'izz (2)	The Devil Preaches	1979	
Ra'aytu fi ma yara al-na'im	I Saw in a Dream	1982	

al-Tanzim al-sirri	The Secret Organisation	1984
Sabah al-ward	Good Morning to You	1987
al-Fajr al-kadhib	The False Dawn	1989
al-Qarar al-akhir	The Final Decision	1996
Sada al-nisyan	Echo of Oblivion	1999

Other Kinds of Narrative

| Asda' al-sira al-dhatiya | Echoes of an Autobiography | 1994 |
| Ahlam fatrat al-naqaha | The Dreams and Dreams of Departure | 2006 |

Mahfouz gave hundreds of interviews during his long life. A valuable and insightful selection published under his name, edited by Sabri Hafiz, continues to be *Atahaddath ilaykum* (I Say to You) (Beirut: 1977).

The nearest thing to memoirs published by Mahfouz are two books, both consisting of long taped conversations with other literary figures who then produced approved books out of them. The first was done by the novelist Jamal al-Ghitani under the title, *Naguib Mahfouz yatadhakkar* (Naguib Mahfouz Remembers) (Beirut: 1980); republished with a long introduction by Ghitani (Cairo: 1987); re-titled and published with much additional material as *al-Majalis al-mahfuziya* (*The Mahfouz Dialogues*) (Cairo: 2006). The second was compiled by critic Raja' al-Naqqash, titled *Naguib Mahfouz: safahat min mudhakkiratih wa adwa' jadida 'ala adabih wa hayatih* (Naguib Mahfouz: Pages from his Memoirs and a New Light Shed on his Literature and Life) (Cairo: 1998).

Mahfouz's journalism, consisting mostly of a very short weekly column published in *al-Ahram* from the mid-1970s until his death, has largely been collected in nine volumes, edited by Fathi al-'Ashri, and published by al-Dar al-Misriya al-Lubnaniya in Cairo between the years 1990–2003. The collections cover the following topics in order of publication: 'Religion and Democracy', 'Culture and Education', 'Youth and Freedom', 'Religion and Extremism', 'Law and Justice', 'Arabs and Arabism', 'Science and Work', 'Freedom and Progress' and 'Literature and Philosophy'. A good selection in English is that prepared by Mohamed Salmawy, *Reflections of a Nobel Laureate, 1994–2001* (Cairo: 2001).

Mahfouz in English Translation

In addition to the 31 italicised titles under 'Novels', 'Other Kinds of Narrative' and 'Journalism' above, several selections from the short stories and plays of Mahfouz are also available in English as follows. It must be noted that none of the collections in English is a complete translation of any single Arabic collection as published by Mahfouz. Rather, they are their own translators' selections from any number of Mahfouz's original collections. Unless otherwise stated, all the English translations listed above or below are currently published by the American University Press in Cairo.

God's World (Bibliotheca Islamica, Minneapolis: 1973);
One-Act Plays I (General Egyptian Book Organisation, Cairo: 1989)
    (Contains four out of Mahfouz's eight one-act plays);
The Time and the Place and Other Stories (1991);
The Seventh Heaven: Stories of the Supernatural (2005);
Voices from the Other World: Ancient Egyptian Tales (2006).

It is worth noting also that a number of stories other than in the above collections have been translated and remain scattered in a wide variety of publications.

Further Reading

The following list in no way aims at being comprehensive. It does not list all books on Mahfouz, nor does it take account of articles in periodicals, chapters in books, or unpublished dissertations and theses, of all of which copious material exists in both Arabic and English. Finally, not all the contents of this list have necessarily been referred to in the text of the present book. On the other hand, works fully referenced in the Notes are not re-listed here.

In English

Jad, Ali B, *Form and Technique in the Egyptian Novel: 1912–1971* (Ithaca Press, Reading: 1983). Perceptive and comprehensive up to 1971.

Moosa, Matti, *The Origins of Modern Arabic Fiction* (Lynne Rienner Publishers, Boulder, Colo., 2nd revised edition: 1997). On the evolution of the genre of the novel in Arabic literature. Well-researched and highly informative.

Readers who want to view the evolution of the genre of the novel in Arabic within the wider context of the development of other literary genres can consult

Allen, Roger, *The Arabic literary heritage : the development of its genres and criticism* (CUP, Cambridge: 1998);

Badawi, M M, *A Short History of Modern Arabic Literature* (Clarendon Press, Oxford: 1993);

Starkey, Paul, *Modern Arabic Literature* (EUP, Edinburgh: 2006).

Full-length books on Mahfouz

Beard, Michael and Adnan Haydar (eds), *Naguib Mahfouz: from Regional Fame to Global Recognition* (Syracuse University Press, Syracuse, N.Y.: 1993). A collection of previously published articles covering roughly the first half of Mahfouz's career.

El-Enany, Rasheed, *Naguib Mahfouz: the Pursuit of Meaning* (Routledge, London and New York: 1993). The present author's earlier study of Mahfouz and a main source for the current one. Readers wanting a more in-depth look into Mahfouz's work up to 1990 should refer to it.

Le Gassick, Trevor (ed), *Critical Perspectives on Naguib Mahfouz* (Three Continents Press, Washington D.C.: 1991). A collection of previously published articles, mostly originally written in English but some translated from Arabic by the editor. Deals with a selection of Mahfouz's works up to the early 1970s.

Milson, Menahem, *Najib Mahfuz: the Novelist-Philosopher of Cairo* (St Martin's Press, New York: 1998). Inevitably repetitive of earlier work but contains useful insights into the aesthetics of Mahfouz's work.

Moosa, Matti, *The Early Novels of Naguib Mahfouz: Images of Modern Egypt* (University Press of Florida, Gainesville, Fla: 1994). Despite publication date, only deals with Mahfouz's output until 1959.

Peled, Mattityahu, *Religion My Own: the Literary Works of Najib Mahfuz* (Transaction Books, New Brunswick: 1983). Accords more importance to Mahfouz's early historical novels than other critics have done, looking at them in terms of utopian fiction. Analyses and conclusions are intellectually engaging but tend sometimes to coerce Mahfouz's work into a preconceived pattern. Considers Mahfouz's work up to the late 1960s.

Somekh, Sasson, *The Changing Rhythm: a Study of Najib Mahfuz's Novels* (E J Brill, Leiden: 1973). Methodical and perceptive. Contains a useful introductory chapter outlining the state of the Egyptian novel before Mahfouz's arrival on the scene. Deals with Mahfouz's fiction up to the late 1960s.

In Arabic

Ghali Shukri, *al-Muntami* (The Nonconformist) (Cairo, 2nd edition: 1969). A socio-political reading of Mahfouz through a Marxist-cum-existentialist perspective. Sprawling and undisciplined but can be rewarding sometimes. Deals with Mahfouz's work up to the late 1960s.

Mahmud Amin al-'Alim, *Ta'ammulat fi 'alam Naguib Mahfouz* (Reflections on the World of Naguib Mahfouz) (Cairo: 1970). Unmethodical but highly revealing forays into the work of Mahfouz. Author's approach based on study of structure as a unifying element both within single works and in their totality. Illustrates the possible reward of such an approach but does not go on to carry it out on the extensive scale it would require. Stops at end of the 1960s.

Jurj Tarabishi, *Allah fi rihlat Naguib Mahfouz al-ramziyya* (God in the Symbolic Works of Naguib Mahfouz) (Beirut, 3rd edition: 1980; first published in 1973). A penetrating and lucidly argued analysis of Mahfouz's metaphysical quest in a number of novels and short stories from *Children of the Alley* to *A Tale without Beginning or End*.

'Abd al-Muhsin Taha Badr, *Naguib Mahfouz: al-ru'ya wa-l-adat* (Naguib Mahfouz: Vision and Technique) (Cairo: 1978). A methodical and elaborate study by a seasoned academic; probably the best-researched on its subject in Arabic. A class-conscious reading of Mahfouz with meticulous and rigorous observation of the development of the novelist's craft and prose style. Invaluable for the analysis and bibliographical account of Mahfouz's early uncollected essays and short stories. Intolerant of Mahfouz's fatalistic view of life and occasionally harsh in tone – quite unusual, since Mahfouz has rarely met with anything but acclaim from his critics. It is very unfortunate that this book (originally intended as Volume 1 of a comprehensive study) has never been completed. Its detailed and systematic consideration (485 pages) of Mahfouz's work proceeds no further than *The Beginning and the End,* published in 1949.

'Ali Shalash, *Naguib Mahfouz: al-tariq wa-l-sada* (Naguib Mahfouz: the Road and the Echo) (Beirut: 1990). Informative on the early critical reception of Mahfouz before *The Trilogy* established his fame. Includes in an appendix the full text of 14 early reviews of Mahfouz's work.

Siza Ahmad Qasim, *Bina' al-riwaya: dirasa muqarana li thulathiyyat Naguib Mahfouz* (The Structure of the Novel: a Comparative Study of Mahfouz's *Trilogy*) (Cairo: 1984). A structuralist approach to *The Cairo Trilogy.* Often reads like a manual in retrospect for the writing of the novel but hardly any attempt at putting it in the service of interpretation. Perhaps its strongest point is in the comparisons with masters of European realism such as Balzac and Flaubert which go to prove that by the time of *The Trilogy* Mahfouz had already transcended classical realism and embarked on techniques of modernism.

Picture Sources

The author and publishers wish to express their thanks to the following sources of illustrative material and/or permission to reproduce it. They will make proper acknowledgements in future editions in the event that any omissions have occurred.

The American University in Cairo Press: 14, 36, 39, 56.
al-Ahram Archive: iii, 49, 54, 75, 87, 112, 151, 153, 156.
Egypt Historical Archive: 26.

Index

NB All family relationships are to Naguib Mahfouz.